"That leaves Lee and Brigit."

John's face tightened. "They can both read."

"We have to trust them." Emily looked from John to Duncan and back again as she asserted, "I do, I'm telling you."

Duncan shoved his hands in his pockets. It had to be Lee then. His sweet little Brigit wouldn't ever—

John forged ahead. "I've been trying to put the facts together. Lee was gone on her days off when the locket and cameo were taken. That leaves Brigit."

Sick anger washed over Duncan. *I trusted the lass. I was ready to make her my wife. How could I have been such an idiot? She's been playing me for a fool all this time.* She'd been clever and quick about helping him over a rough spot or two with Emily's matchmaking—but now he realized she might well be a woman accustomed to keeping secrets. 'Twas also a way she turned him into an ally so he'd drop his guard and not be suspicious. Oh—and that habit she had of slipping her hand into her apron pocket that he'd thought was so endearing— was it a sinister thing? Had she been swiping things from under his very nose?

CATHY MARIE HAKE is a southern California native who loves her work as a nurse and Lamaze teacher. She and her husband have a daughter, a son, and two dogs, so life is never dull or quiet. Cathy considers herself a sentimental packrat, collecting antiques and Hummel figurines. She otherwise keeps busy with reading, writing, baking, and being a prayer warrior. "I am easily distracted during prayer, so I devote certain tasks and chores to specific requests or persons so I can keep faithful in my prayer life." Contact Cathy at her website: www.CathyMarieHake.com

Books by Cathy Marie Hake

HEARTSONG PRESENTS
HP370—Twin Victories
HP481—Unexpected Delivery
HP512—Precious Burdens
HP545—Love Is Patient

Redeemed Hearts

Cathy Marie Hake

Heartsong Presents

To my readers, who share with me in the faith, hopes, and dreams of real life and still spend time to turn the pages of my books. God bless you!

A note from the Author:
I love to hear from my readers! You may correspond with me by writing:

> **Cathy Marie Hake**
> **Author Relations**
> **PO Box 719**
> **Uhrichsville, OH 44683**

ISBN 1-59310-105-8

REDEEMED HEARTS

Our mission is to publish and distribute inspirational products offering exceptional value and biblical encouragement to the masses.

All of the characters and events in this book are fictitious. Any resemblance to actual persons, living or dead, or to actual events is purely coincidental.

All Scripture quotations are taken from the King James Version of the Bible.

PRINTED IN THE U.S.A.

one

Virginia, October 1860

"Aye, now, you're a beauty, to be sure." Duncan O'Brien reached out and caressed the sleek hull. Sawdust, pine tar, and salty air mingled to add to the sense of rightness. He'd just come back from a voyage and resolutely seen to the usual captain's duties before hastening here. Newcomb Shipping boasted a shipyard all its own. The vessel currently under construction would belong to him.

"We're making good progress," John Newcomb, his much older brother-in-law commented as he slapped an open palm against a sturdy-looking bulwark.

Duncan moved about the dry dock with ease, sidestepping piles of lumber, ducking when wenched loads swung overhead, and striding up a plank to reach the deck. John followed right behind him.

Duncan looked about and grinned. "You were modest in saying you've made good progress. She's at least a month ahead of schedule!"

"It'll be a few months yet ere she's seaworthy. The framework is sound, and the men tell me the timber is cooperative. Old Kemper declares the last time he had a ship put itself together this easily was when he built it inside a bottle."

"Old Kemper? If he says so, that makes it even more remarkable." Duncan didn't bother to hide his smile. The master shipbuilder had cultivated a reputation for being surly. Indeed he had scowling down to a fine art. In the fifty

5

years he'd been in charge of shipbuilding, Kemper winnowed through many a carpenter to form the team that strove for perfection. As a result, Newcomb Shipping earned local fame for the vessels they turned out. Duncan reverently traced a joist. "This lady is a work of art."

"You'd be one to recognize that fact." John clapped a hand on Duncan's shoulder. "I doubt any other captain ever spent half as much time with the construction part of the trade."

"I paid my dues." Duncan nodded with mock solemnity. "It cost me half a licorice rope. The day I shared that rope, Old Kemper transformed into the best mentor a landlubber boy ever met."

John's eyes widened. "Is that what softened the crusty old man?"

"You tellin' tales again?" Old Kemper swaggered up. He shook his finger at Duncan. "How am I to command my men effectively if you reveal my weakness?"

"You earned their respect. That's all you need." Duncan slipped his hand in his pocket and pulled out a twist of paper. He palmed it to Kemper when they shook hands.

"You're a good man, Duncan O'Brien." Old Kemper made no attempt to conceal his gift. He tugged open an end of the paper, popped one of the dime-sized, chewy, black candy "coins" into his mouth, and twisted the paper shut once again. As he tucked the remainder of the licorice into his vest pocket without offering to share, he added, "And I'm not."

They toured the vessel and inspected every last inch. Afterward the three men headed toward the office. Once they finished reviewing the blueprints, Kemper hobbled off. John knocked his knuckles on the plans that lay across his desk. "You'll need to come up with a name for her soon."

"I seem to recall you didn't determine a name for the *Contentment* until the day before she was christened. I figure the right name will come to me in time."

"Well, well. I see you've truly outgrown your impulsiveness," John teased as he rolled up the plans and secured them in his desk.

"Probably not entirely. The responsibilities of captaining your grand vessels and crews have taught me the wisdom of paying consideration to actions and weighing decisions instead of trying to patch up mistakes. The ocean is apt to claim souls for any errors."

"Anticipating and solving problems in advance is a lesson a man learns more than once." John glanced at the clock in the corner. "Speaking of learning lessons—I know better than to disappoint my wife when she plans a special family supper. The last few evenings, I've had meetings. We'd best get going."

Duncan hefted his duffel bag and accompanied his brother-in-law out of the office. Duncan was a man who straddled two lives. One foot belonged aboard a deck; the other belonged on land where a loving family welcomed him with open arms. He counted himself blessed—a man couldn't hope for more than to be at ease with his family and his calling.

❧

Brigit Murphy heard a giggle. She glanced over her shoulder and gave Trudy a questioning look.

"I tied me pinafore a wee bit tighter." Trudy proceeded to dampen her fingertips and smooth back a few stray wisps of her ginger-colored hair. "Miss Emily's brother just got home, and I'm wanting to look my best for him."

Brigit shook her head in disbelief. What would make a simple maid like Trudy think a man of distinction might give a fleeting thought to courting her? Such thinking led to pure folly.

Trudy had hired on only a month before her, but she was younger and of a more outgoing nature.

"Trudy, no maid ever keeps a position once her reputation comes under scrutiny," Brigit whispered, "even when 'tisn't her fault. Please—"

Trudy's lips pushed into a spoiled moue. "Oh, your mood's as black as your hair. You wouldn't be such a stick-in-the-mud if you knew Miss Emily was a cleaning woman afore she married Mr. John. What's wrong with a girl like me wishing for the same good luck? Besides, once you see this strapping man, you'll be trying to catch his attention, too. Why, Duncan O'Brien's the most dashing sea captain a lass ever saw!"

"I'm not about to chase after a man. Go on ahead and set your own cap for him."

Trudy waggled her brows. "Not that I'd mind catching the likes of Miss Emily's brother, but what cap?"

Laughter bubbled out of Brigit. The lady of the house didn't make her staff wear caps. In fact, Miss Emily didn't dress her maids in black, either. Shrugging at convention, Miss Emily ran her home in a unique manner. Cornflower blue dresses and rotating work assignments kept the maids a merry bunch. None of the maids held a permanent assignment—Brigit was just as likely to be asked to polish the silver or sweep out a grate as she was to be dusting the master's bedchamber or minding the children. In fact, in the two weeks Brigit had been employed here, she'd seen Miss Emily don an apron and teach her oldest two daughters how to bake bread!

Taking care to tie her ruffled serving pinafore rather loosely, Brigit hummed appreciatively at the aroma filling the air as Cook opened the oven. Roast beef. Until she'd come to work here, Brigit hadn't tasted roast in at least four years. Another of the Newcombs' quirks was that the staff enjoyed the same entrees as the family. Miss Emily said it made for less work for the cook, but everyone knew better. The staff adored their mistress and took pleasure in telling Brigit from the very first day that Miss Emily once held a job as a lowly servant and never assumed airs. Clearly she commanded her household by dint of affection, and it ran seamlessly.

Brigit knew the details of running a large mansion. As a landowner's daughter back in Ireland, she'd been reared with the expectation that she'd wed a well-to-do gentleman and manage his home. Mum saw to training her well. Then the famine hit. The blight on the crops rated as a horrible disaster, but Da always subscribed to the revelation of Joseph's dream in the Old Testament and saved for lean times. Year after year things worsened. Farmers left for the New World. Many of the house servants were wives, sisters, and daughters who went along. Brigit and Mum took over the chores.

Never once had they bemoaned the change in circumstances. Saint Paul's words from the fourth chapter of Philippians became the Murphy family's credo: "For I have learned, in whatsoever state I am, therewith to be content. I know both how to be abased, and I know how to abound: every where and in all things I am instructed both to be full and to be hungry, both to abound and to suffer need. I can do all things through Christ which strengtheneth me." Even now, after they'd come to America and her parents lived in a tenement, Brigit willingly took on the role of a servant. She felt God's presence in her life and counted her blessings. Tonight one of those blessings would be roast beef.

Trudy nudged her. "Just you wait and see. Now that Duncan O'Brien is home, there'll be a parade of eligible girls coming through the door. He usually manages to talk Mr. John into sending him off on a voyage when the ladies start batting their lashes at him." She pinched her cheeks to bring up some color. "It'll be different this time."

Cook started carving the roast and missed Trudy's primping actions. "Aye, that it will," she said. "Trudy, dish up the carrots. Brigit, grab the pitcher of milk." As if she hadn't given the instructions, she continued. "I heard Miss Emily tell Mr. John it's high time she found her brother a wife."

Goodhew, the butler, wagged his finger. "Keep quiet about him for now. Mr. John wanted Duncan's arrival to be a surprise for Miss Emily."

Cook batted away Goodhew's finger and gave him a peck on the cheek. Anywhere else in the house, they conducted themselves according to their station; but in the kitchen, they switched back into a happily married couple. "It won't be much of a surprise. I had Fiona set a place at the table for Duncan."

Goodhew tugged on his coat sleeve. "Miss Emily will be so busy attending the children, she won't notice an extra plate. Mark my word, as long as no one says a thing, she'll be surprised."

Cook picked up her carving knife again. "Be that as it may, the real surprise will be on that young man. If he sets sail again without being pledged to marry, I'll polish every last piece of silver in this house myself."

Trudy and the other maid, Lee, exchanged looks. "Who do you think—"

Brigit took the milk and gladly escaped to the dining room. She didn't want to overhear the gossip. Then again, she did. In an odd way everyone on the Newcomb estate was like a family. Oh, to be sure, she knew it wasn't anything close to the truth—but the kindhearted close-knit group of servants had made her feel welcome at once. Aye, and Miss Emily never once said a harsh word. More telling still—Miss Emily herself usually minded the children, but if she was busy, she directed Brigit to look after the lasses. The Lord's way of providing this position for her couldn't be more clear. A few tales wouldn't be harmful, but Brigit didn't want to risk stepping over the line and jeopardizing her job.

"Dinner is served," Brigit overheard Goodhew say. She quickly finished pouring a glass of milk, then scooted to the side and kept her back to the wall. She'd learned the Newcomb tribe didn't waste time reaching the table. At eleven, Titus had the gangly legs of a pony. He galloped in ahead of six-year-old Phillip. Both had their mother's bright red hair. The five-year-old twins bumped into each other as they spilled through the doorway. June shrieked, and Julie giggled. They scrambled into their seats while Anna Kathleen and Lily tried to make more ladylike appearances. At thirteen and ten, they'd both just been warned to act less like hooligans, or their father threatened to cut off their lovely dark brown curls so they'd look like boys. Timothy came in, somber as a priest. At fourteen, he seemed far older than his years. Miss Emily smoothly swiped the book he carried and set it on the buffet before Goodhew seated her. Mr. John came in and gave her a kiss on the cheek, then took his own seat.

"I'm so glad you made it to supper tonight," Miss Emily said, smiling at her husband.

"Are you glad I made it to supper, too?" a deep voice asked from the doorway.

Miss Emily let out a cry of delight, popped up, and dashed over to the tall young man. His auburn curls picked up the lamplight and looked like polished copper. Laughter shone in his bright blue eyes. He lifted Emily and swung her around, then set her down and gave her a kiss on the cheek. "That makes it official. I'm home."

As he dragged another chair over to the table, Duncan started teasing the children. "I have things in my duffel bag, but only for kids who eat their vegetables."

Trudy brought in the carrots, Cook delivered the roast, and the other two maids followed in their wake with a basket of hot rolls and braised potatoes. Brigit filled the rest of the children's glasses and turned to leave, but the stranger halted her motion by resting his large, rough hand on her wrist. Startlingly blue eyes twinkled at her.

Duncan wore the smile of a rascal. "Don't I get any milk?"

Is he teasing me? She pasted on an uncertain smile. "If you're wanting some, Sir."

"Aye. Some say 'tis a drink for the young, but it suits me just fine."

As she reached for his glass, Brigit wondered why he drank milk, of all things. It must not be an unusual thing, after all, because when Fiona had set Duncan O'Brien's place at the table, she'd provided him with a glass as well as a coffee cup.

"Brigit," Miss Emily said merrily, "that's my little brother, Duncan, back from a voyage. He's a bit of a scamp and a tease at times, but he truly does like milk."

Duncan's brows lifted. "Little brother? Emily, you may be older, but you're the minnow in the family net."

While everyone at the table chattered, Brigit poured milk for the handsome sea captain and scurried back into the kitchen.

Trudy stood in the middle of the kitchen with her hands theatrically clasped over her heart. "Oh, just the sight of him makes me heart flutter. That man can sweep me off me feet any day."

Unaccustomed to the familiarity the staff displayed toward the family, Brigit busied herself with washing some pots and pans. Lee grabbed a dish towel and started drying. Cook came over and slipped another pan into the sink and let out a sigh. "You lasses keep an eye on Trudy. She wouldn't know proper conduct if she tripped on it, and she's liable to make a ninny of herself over Duncan."

"She wouldn't be the first woman ever to do that," Lee whispered.

"No, she wouldn't, but the others have stood a faint chance of actually qualifying as wife material. They all hailed from good families—not from the servants' quarters."

Brigit didn't marvel that women were attracted to Duncan's fine looks and rakish smile. Aye, and he'd be a good provider, too. He'd be a fine fellow for a lass to contemplate marrying, but any man who captained a vessel wouldn't be the type to sit back and let others do his matchmaking.

Miss Emily qualified as a force with which to be reckoned, and she had her mind set to play Cupid. If Duncan were half as adamant to remain single, things would be downright entertaining around the Newcomb estate.

Trudy primped in front of the tiny mirror over the washstand. "I mightn't be a ravishing beauty, but plenty a man's told me I'm fair pretty. Me mum always said, 'All's fair in love and war.'"

Lee snorted. "You'd best count on war, not love, Trudy."

Cook propped her hands on her ample hips and scowled. "You'll not be dallying with Duncan, do you hear me? It's not proper, and this is a proper home. Miss Emily's determined to marry her brother off to a nice young lady, and he deserves more than a servant who can't read her own name."

Brigit nodded her agreement. God was no respecter of persons, but man surely was. Common sense dictated a man of Duncan O'Brien's station wed a woman whose abilities allowed her to be his helpmeet. Servants were servants, even in America. Brigit Murphy expected no prince to sweep her anywhere. She grabbed the broom and set to work. The only thing getting swept around her was the floor.

two

"I'll likely be here for three weeks, if you can stand me," Duncan answered his sister's query. "I need to see about several of the details on the ship."

"Which ship?" June asked.

"The ship he's building with Old Kemper," Titus scoffed. "Everyone knows the ship that's most important to a man is the one he calls his own."

Duncan shook his head. "Nae, Lad. The most important ship to a man is the one he's captaining at any given moment. He's responsible for all souls on board, whether or not the papers say the vessel belongs to him."

John stared at Timothy, Titus, and Phillip. "You boys heed your uncle Duncan's words. That sense of responsibility and duty are why he's the youngest captain in my fleet."

"Dad, I want to go on a voyage," Timothy declared. "It's well past time."

"Me, too," Titus chimed in. "Uncle Duncan was going to sea by the time he was eleven."

Duncan gave the boys a long, hard look. "'Twas a different time and different circumstances." He didn't enlarge on the particulars. The family took care not to make references to the period surrounding Timothy's birth. Duncan had been a wee lad, but he'd had to grow up fast. With Emily working all hours to provide for them, he'd tried to help his dying sister, Anna, with her baby son until John rescued them all.

A faint red crept from Timothy's neck up to his hairline. Though his nephew never said a word about it, Duncan knew he was sensitive about the fact that his mother's marriage to

John's brother, Edward, had been a sham; and his own birth eventually cost his mother her life.

Duncan cleared his throat and winked. "I've been talking to your father." He glanced at John. John was really Timothy's uncle; but for the sake of ease and love, he and Emily called themselves his parents. "I've tried to convince him to let the both of you go out with me on a voyage."

"Hurrah!" Tim and Titus both straightened up.

"Hold on for a moment," Emily cut in.

Duncan caught on that John hadn't spoken with Emily yet. "Oops. It seems I've let the cat out of the bag too soon. Now, our Em, surely you can see for yourself that these fine sons of yours are growing—"

"What I can see is that my brother and my husband are trying to pull the wool over my eyes." She gave him a stern look. "Not another word out of you, Duncan O'Brien, if you value your life."

"Em—"

"I said, not another word!"

He couldn't hide his grin as he gave out a dramatic sigh, then muttered, "I was just going to ask for the salt."

John took up the cudgels. "How are you boys doing with your lessons?"

"I'm a full year ahead in my studies," Timothy declared. "And I've mastered every knot you and Duncan taught me."

"Me, too!" Titus wasn't about to be left out.

Duncan hid a smile behind the rim of his cup. Titus made up for his lack of size with an abundance of spunk. Emily would have a conniption if she knew he'd let both of the boys climb up the mast of the *Cormorant* last time he was in dock; but his nephews had salt water flowing in their veins, and it did them good to use their muscles every bit as much as they used their brains.

"So you have me slated to go to the Boott Mills in

Massachusetts this next trip?" Duncan gave John a conspiratorial look.

"Aye, that I do. Aunt Mildred lives up there."

"I'd like to visit her," Anna Kathleen declared.

Emily set her knife and fork on her plate. Her eyes glittered dangerously. "I'll not be badgered into any decision. Anna Kathleen, you're too young to travel alone; and, no, Lily, you going along would not make it any better. Tim and Titus, stop elbowing one another. You'll be black and blue by the time supper's over. I've a good three weeks to watch your behavior, and I'll take every last day of them before I make up my mind whether or not to let you go. Don't any of you dare try to bully me into anything. I'll not stand for it."

After supper was over, Emily dismissed the children from the table. Duncan and John remained behind with her to enjoy a cup of after-dinner coffee. Emily's eyes took on an appraising light, and Duncan felt the hair on the back of his neck prickle.

"So you'll be twenty-one in a few months."

"Aye, Em. We all know that."

"Yes, well, I'm assessing facts, as I said. I'm thinkin' it's well past time for you to find a pretty little wi—"

"Cast that thought aside!" Duncan's coffee cup thumped down on the table. "I've many a year left of bachelorhood."

"You'd do well with a woman to settle you."

"The only thing unsettling me is this crazy notion of yours. Em, don't try to play Cupid for me. When I'm good and ready, I'll find my own wife—and not a day before."

"There's no harm in my making introductions." Emily took a sip and gave him a pointed look over the brim of her cup. "You'll never find a sweetheart when you spend all your time at the docks or at sea, so I'm going to help out a bit."

Duncan rose and shook his head. "John, talk some sense into her."

To Duncan's dismay, John reached over and held his wife's hand. "Emily's always carried a full cargo of common sense."

"You'd best check the manifest and take inventory." Duncan tapped his head as he went out the door. "She's got a couple of empty crates in the upper cabin."

≈

Brigit sat in the balcony of the church and kept her attention on the preacher. The yawn she hid behind her hand didn't reflect on his message—the blame ought to land directly on Trudy's shoulders. She'd been unable to sleep last night, so she'd come into Brigit's attic bedroom and mooned over the dashing young sea captain.

Brigit spent more than half the night trying to talk some reason into her flighty friend. Her admonishments went in one ear and out the other. Trudy showed up for church this morning with an elaborate hairstyle she vowed would earn her Duncan's attention. Instead, Duncan sat with his family down below in the sanctuary, completely oblivious to the fact that he'd been the inspiration for such a creation. Then again Trudy didn't suffer from his inattention. She'd fallen asleep.

The Newcomb household ran with flawless precision, thanks to Goodhew's discipline. Five minutes after the benediction, the servants took a carriage back to the mansion so they could put out changes of clothing for the children and have a meal ready to set on the table. Because she'd been assigned to travel with the children today, Brigit didn't go along with the rest of the staff.

She stood to the side of the children's carriage and minded June and Julie while Anna Kathleen and Lily took their places across from Titus and Phillip. Normally one of the maids and the younger children took one carriage while Mr. John and Miss Emily took Timothy and Anna Kathleen with them in the other. Today they'd been supplanted by Duncan—which might have been tolerable—but now Mr.

John gallantly assisted a young woman into the carriage who settled into the space Timothy or Anna might have occupied. The young woman graced Mr. John with a thankful nod, then turned a dazzling smile on Duncan and patted the seat next to her.

Brigit ignored Timothy and Anna's mutinous expressions and let go of Julie's hand so the groom could lift the child into the wagon. June didn't wait—she scrambled up unassisted. A tangle of too many arms and legs filled the carriage, and Brigit had yet to take a seat. Just as she daintily lifted her hem, a deep voice said from behind her, "Hold now. This cannot be."

"Unca Duncan, ride with us!" Phillip's face lit up.

Duncan chortled. "This vessel appears to have plenty of bulk, but no ballast. I'm going to have to trim the load a bit. Phillip, dive over to me. Lily, be a good girl and come here. You can each ride with us in the other carriage."

"This isn't fair," Anna Kathleen protested.

Duncan gave Phillip and Lily a gentle push toward the other conveyance, then rested his forearms on the edge of the carriage. "No, 'tisn't. Many's the time you'll do what's required of you rather than what you want. Fair is nothing more than a child's justice or a weather prediction."

Brigit found his words quite true, and he spoke them with both certainty and a tinge of humor. She waited for him to move to the side. As he did, he took her hand and helped her into the carriage with all of the care and polish he'd employ with a high-society lass. Aye, he was a gentleman through and through.

❧

Duncan strode back and took a seat beside Phillip. He gave brief consideration to holding his nephew on his lap since Miss Prudence Carston's extravagant hoops took up an inordinate amount of space. Miss Carston pasted on a smile and batted her lashes, but Duncan could tell she found no delight at a lad sitting between them. Manners forced her to feign amusement, but the young woman's lack of sincerity registered as plainly as a loudly luffing sail.

He'd told Emily not to try her hand at matchmaking, and this opening salvo had best also be the final one.

Phillip's nose twitched. "You smell like flowers."

Miss Carston preened. It might well take her half of eternity if she fluffed all the ruffles on her dress. "Roses. I always wear roses. I think they go well with my favorite color."

"I like pink, too," Lily said in an awestruck tone.

"Aren't you fortunate you inherited your papa's dark hair then? Redheaded women simply cannot wear pink." Miss Carston turned to Duncan. She artfully brushed a few tendrils by the brim of her hat. The hat looked remarkably like a pink iced cake, and her lace-gloved hand resembled a fussy, tatted doily. The whole while, she studied his hair. "I hope you won't consider me too forward to say your jacket looks quite dashing with your auburn hair."

Forward? Aye, that she was. And insipid as could be. Men didn't take into account such trifling matters; furthermore, every last man in the congregation wore a black coat! This paragon of pink might well have Emily's approval, but she left Duncan cold as a mackerel at midnight. As soon as they finished luncheon, he'd concoct a polite reason to slip away— if he survived that long.

John helped Emily into the carriage and took his place, then drove toward home. Emily tried to spark a conversation, and Miss Carston plunged in with notable enthusiasm. Duncan held his tongue. He didn't want to be a surly beast, but the last thing he needed was for social nicety to be mistaken for interest. He refused to lead a woman into hoping for church bells when the only chime he heard was freedom's ring.

Once home, Duncan assisted Emily's candidate out of the carriage. Little Phillip, bless his soul, didn't appreciate the finer points of conduct and let out a whoop as he jumped onto Duncan's back. "Gimme a piggyback ride into the house, Unca Duncan!"

"Sure, little man." Duncan grinned at the young lady, who managed to quickly hide her look of shock. "We're an informal bunch at home, Miss Carston."

"How lovely. Far be it from me to spoil such leisurely comfort with formality. Please do call me Prudence."

While Emily and Brigit shepherded the children upstairs to change before lunch, Duncan suffered the necessary indignity of entertaining Emily's guest. She laced her hand into the crook of his arm and glided alongside him into the large parlor. Inspiration struck. He tilted his head toward the piano. "Do you play?"

"Modestly." The humble response might have come across more sincerely if she hadn't let loose of him and hastened to the bench. After limbering her fingers with a few scales, she folded her hands in her lap. "Oh. It's Sunday."

"Yes, it is."

"Papa allows only hymns on Sunday. He says on the Lord's day we ought only play and sing unto the Almighty."

"I can respect that." Duncan wondered why that presented a problem. "Why don't you play a hymn?"

A faint blush filled her cheeks. "I don't see a hymnal. Everyone else is able to play from memory, but I can't seem to recall the particulars of any piece, myself."

"Anna and Lily both take lessons. I'm sure there must be music in the bench." The minute he made that offer, Duncan knew he'd said the wrong thing. Prudence's face turned an unbecoming color, and her eyes flashed.

"I said I played modestly well. I'm not a novice." The words barely left her mouth, and she teared up. "Oh, I'm so sorry. How dreadfully rude of me. You didn't mean any insult, I'm sure."

Unmoved by her emotional show, Duncan continued to prop his elbow on the piano and gave her a bland look. Prudence managed to display a wide range of coy tricks. She'd tried charm, meekness, tolerance, friendliness, humility, temper, and tears. If he didn't miss his guess, ploys for sympathy and something to induce obligation or guilt weren't far behind. Tedious. The whole matter bored him to distraction. Instead of hastening to reassure her she'd not spoken amiss, he glanced down at the ivory keys.

"Anna's impetuous, but it puts fire behind her playing. As for Lily—she shows talent far beyond her age."

"How nice." Prudence dabbed at her cheeks with a lacy hanky, then looked up at him through her lashes. "Do you play?"

"Very badly."

"But you do so many other things well. Why, everyone knows you're the youngest captain around, and soon you'll even own your own boat!"

Boat. He inwardly winced. Calling his grand ship a boat would be like labeling Notre Dame a chapel.

*

"We'll walk downstairs like ladies," Brigit said to the Newcomb girls. Anna lifted her head and drew back her shoulders a shade; then Brigit nodded her approval. "Very nice. June and Julie, walk—don't bounce."

Lily clutched Brigit's hand. "It's not bad manners, is it— that I'm wearing pink, too?"

"Not at all. You look very pretty." All the girls were eager to get downstairs and be with Duncan and his guest, so it hadn't taken them long to change. Most children ate Sunday dinner in their church clothes, but Miss Emily wouldn't hear of it. She insisted best clothing ought to stay nice; and after watching the twins' predilection for spilling food, Brigit understood why. As soon as she installed the girls in the parlor, she'd go tie on an apron and help Cook serve the ham.

When they reached the entryway, Brigit could see over the girls' heads. Miss Prudence Carston looked happy as a bee in honeysuckle; Duncan looked as if he'd just been stung. As soon as he heard the girls, he spun around and beckoned. "I just boasted to Miss Carston about your talent on the piano. Come play a tune for her."

Miss Carston stood and promptly sidled up to him. "Yes, darlings. Come play for us. We'd love to hear you."

Customarily, Julie and June would romp outside for a short while, but since Brigit could hear Mr. and Mrs. Newcomb approaching, and they had a luncheon guest, she knew the girls should remain inside. Brigit turned away and slipped into the kitchen. As she tied on her apron, she looked about to determine where her help was most needed.

"Have you ever seen a better ham?" Cook beamed at the platter she held.

"Virginia ham," Brigit said in an appreciative tone as she dodged Lee, who carried a pan of scalloped potatoes.

Trudy dumped green beans into a bowl and scowled. "Killing the fatted calf for Miss Pink-and-Pretty."

"It's pork, not beef," Cook snapped.

"Miss Carston comes from good family," Goodhew added. "I'll go summon them to the table."

Assigned to pour milk again, Brigit filled the children's cups as the family came into the room. She stood back by the buffet as Mr. John said the prayer; then she slipped quietly to Miss Carston's side. "Sweet tea or milk, Miss?"

"Sweet tea, of course." She turned to Duncan. "I declare, just because I'm petite, people treat me as if I'm a child."

Brigit silently filled her glass and proceeded on to the next seat. Duncan smiled at her. "I'll have my usual, Brigit."

As she poured milk for him, Brigit heard Miss Carston's muffled gasp. That gasp then turned into a twitter of a laugh. "Oh, Duncan, aren't you a tease!"

Brigit admired Duncan for his tolerance. What man would appreciate his sister's blatant attempt at matchmaking? Miss Emily and Mr. John both cast appeasing looks at Duncan, but the young Miss Carston chattered on, and Brigit headed for the blessed escape of the kitchen. She strongly suspected Duncan would like to do the same thing.

❧

Three days later Duncan rushed into the library and shut the door behind him. He leaned his head against the door for a moment, then pushed away. He'd appeal to John to talk to Emily. Emily wasn't listening to a word Duncan said, and this simply could not continue. He'd been stuck with Pink Prudence after church on Sunday, then come home last night to supper with Adele-the-Able-Minded, who discussed the Lincoln-Douglas Debates with far more passion than almost any man he'd heard. Now Emily had both of those girls and a few more in the parlor for tea.

He'd ducked in here, hoping to find his way to freedom. The seldom-used door to the garden promised a route of escape—except for the fact that the pretty new raven-haired maid stood over by that very wall, polishing the windows. She glanced at him, then concentrated on her work.

Good. She hadn't spoken. Knowing his luck, Emily might overhear Brigit and come to investigate. Duncan strode toward the exit with all of the resolve of a man swimming toward the only remaining hatch so he could escape a sinking vessel. As he approached, Brigit opened the windowed doors and concentrated on a small streak in one corner. He could see the amusement in her eyes.

The doorknob to the library rattled. He'd never make it through the door and out of sight. Quick as could be, Duncan shot between two bookcases. He gave Brigit a conspiratorial grin, then held a finger to his lips in a silent plea.

"Oh, that brother of mine." Emily sighed from across the room. "He was supposed to come home about now. I thought I heard him come in the front door, but he managed to give me the slip. Did he dash out to the garden?"

"No, Miss Emily."

"This would be so much easier if he'd just cooperate."

Brigit smiled, but Duncan appreciated how she said nothing. Now there was a fine woman. She knew when to hold her tongue, didn't lie, and understood a man needed to tend his own business without interference.

"The windows are impeccable. You've done wonders in this room. Why don't you treat yourself to a book and read for awhile?"

"Why, thank you, Miss Emily!"

Duncan felt a jolt of pleasure. She could read! A great portion of the Irish immigrants were illiterate. So many of the men on his vessels struggled over that very issue. Had he not been so very fortunate with the opportunities afforded him, he'd never have made it this far. Others who weren't as blessed would be stuck without choices if they couldn't read and write. Duncan offered a lesson each day on dock or at sea, and nearly half of his seamen participated.

The door clicked shut, and he waited a moment as he heard his sister cross back to the parlor. "Thank you," he said very softly.

The maid bit her lip, but her shoulders shook a few times, giving her away. Merriment shone in her eyes. "I'll not tell lies for ye."

"I'd not ask you to." He looked at the bookcases all around. The library held an extensive selection, one he considered the greatest material wealth of the home. "What book will you choose?"

She wiped her hands on her apron hem as she looked at the shelves. Anticipation lit her features, adding intriguing depth to her beauty. "I once read *The Last of the Mohicans* by James Fenimore Cooper. Have you any of his other works?"

"*The Prairie* is in here somewhere. I also liked *The Pioneers*." His eyes narrowed as he forced himself to turn and scan the spines. "The fact books are on the side closest to the fireplace. John keeps the fiction books shelved over here. Once upon a time things were alphabetical, but the kids tend to shove the books back in odd spots. I seem to recall that particular set by Cooper was bound in red leather."

Brigit smiled. "Now that'll cut my search down a wee bit, what with the blue, black, and brown covers all ruled out."

"And the green. Don't forget the green."

"Why couldn't it have been pink? That would have been so easy. There are but a handful of those—"

"Pink?" He shuddered. "Spare me. My current association with that hue is less than pleasant."

Brigit dipped her head and started to collect her rags and bucket. The haste with which she acted tickled him. "You've no right to be entertained at my expense, Miss Brigit," Duncan scolded playfully. "I deserve your compassion and pity. If my sister has her way, my single days are sinking as rapidly as a scuttled brigantine with too much ballast."

"So marriage is nothing more than a watery grave?"

He winced. "I'm not ready to get sucked into that whirlpool yet, and when I do, 'twill most assuredly be with the mermaid of my choice—not with Prudence-the-Pink."

"Prudence-the-Pink?" she echoed, her tone carrying an appealing lilt.

Oh, this new maid was a fun-hearted lass—smart as a whip and pretty as a china doll. Duncan chanced a glance toward the door when he heard footsteps and made sure no one was entering. He winked at Brigit and wiped his forehead in a gesture of relief. "Whew. Thought my days were numbered for the second time in a mere hour."

"You've had several more frightening escapades at sea, I'm sure."

"Not at all. There, I am in charge and rely on God. Here, I'm at Emily's mercy—and I fear she has none at all. She's a single-minded woman. Once she sets a course, gale force winds won't stop her."

"Aye, she's a woman of great will and heart."

Just then the faint sounds of a few piano chords sounded, and a screech-toned soprano started to butcher "Rejoice, Rejoice, Believers." Duncan rubbed his temple. "Talk about gales—there you have it! That's an ill wind that blows nobody good."

The lyrics served to underscore just how pathetic the situation had become: "The Bride-groom is a-ris-ing." The soprano proved him right by hitting a combination of shrill notes that sounded just like the bo'sun's cat when a drunken sailor dunked him in the water barrel.

Brigit left the library with her rags and bucket. The sweet sound of laughter she diplomatically squelched before she exited was far more pleasing to his ear.

three

"Duncan! You're whistling 'Rejoice, Rejoice, Believers.'" Miss Emily might well have boiled tea in a pot with the heated look she gave Duncan as he strode into the dining room.

"Why, yes, I am. It's a fine hymn."

Brigit slowly set a basket of rolls on the table and straightened the centerpiece. Truth be told, she didn't want to rush back into the kitchen. A bit of entertainment was brewing, and she wasn't above wanting to watch it unfold. Duncan O'Brien's inadvertent slip was landing him in deep trouble.

Brigit felt an odd kinship with him at that moment, though. All afternoon the same tune nearly drove her daft. Ever since Miss Emily's guest sang that hymn in the parlor while Duncan was making his getaway, Brigit couldn't erase the song from her mind. She'd hummed it, dusted to it, and tapped her fingers in the cadence along the spines of the books in the library until she found the ones Duncan recommended. Now that selfsame song rushed back and netted him.

Emily crossed her arms and tapped her foot impatiently. "Well?"

Miss Emily's shrewd to catch him on that, and he'll not be able to get himself out of this hot water. Boiled Duncan O'Brien for supper.

"All right." Duncan let out a longsuffering sigh. "I'm sorry, Em. It was wrong of me."

"It most certainly was."

Duncan wore the lopsided smile of a charmer whose true repentance was more for saying the apology than for committing the sin. "I shouldn't have done it."

27

"No, you shouldn't," Emily scolded, but her expression softened.

Duncan turned to Timothy, Titus, and Phillip. He gave them a sober look. "Let that be a lesson to you." He paused for a split second, then added, "It is rude to whistle in the house."

Miss Emily let out a squawk. "Duncan, don't you dare try to hoodwink me! You'll tell me why you were whistling that tune here and now."

Brigit headed for the door to the kitchen before her merriment became evident.

"Mama, Brigit was singing it all afternoon," Anna said. "Uncle Duncan must have heard her when he got home."

"Oh, dear." As Brigit turned to the side so she could shoulder the swinging door, she saw color suffuse Miss Emily's face. "Here I was, sure you must've come home and heard Antonia Whalen singing that very song. I'm so sorry, Duncan."

"Talk about sorry," Titus grumbled. "Miss Whalen massacred that song so bad I had to stick my fingers in my ears."

"Yeah. God will have to 'store our hearing after that terr'ble noise," Phillip chimed in.

"That's enough," Emily chided.

Brigit had to bite the inside of her cheek until the door shut and afforded her the safety of the kitchen. She'd heard Miss Whalen's singing, and it'd been more than enough!

Cook fussed over a tray on the table. "Miss Emily may well want to marry up that brother of hers, and I'd be happy as a clam at high tide to bake up a wondrous bridal cake; but will you look at this? Baked my poor fingers to the bone so Miss Emily'd have fine things for them young ladies when they was here this afternoon. We want to entice those young ladies to come visit more often. I put together nice things, and they didn't appreciate the fancy tea I set out one bit."

Lee popped a few crumbs from a piece of chocolate cake into her mouth. "I'd come calling if I'd be served such wondrous fare!"

Less than mollified, Cook grumbled, "Miss Prudence wouldn't eat a bite—and I know it's because she had that corset tied so tight. Miss Adele couldn't very well taste anything because she wouldn't stop yammering over why Mr. Douglas ought to be the next president of these United States."

"She's very well read," Brigit said.

"Reading is fine, but the woman is strident. The Newcomb family table has always been cheerful, and Miss Adele's grating ways would give everyone indigestion." Cook surveyed the kitchen with indignation. "I said I thought Miss Emily's plan to marry off Duncan had merit, but she'd best find better bridal candidates."

Trudy lifted her chin and tapped the center of her chest. "Miss Emily has the right bride here under her verra nose. Serving tea to those rich lasses today near turned me stomach. The Waverly sisters didn't think anyone would notice, but betwixt the pair of them they ate half a raspberry torte."

Cook wagged her head from side to side in a sorrowful manner. "If that wasn't enough, I had to mix up some warm lemonade for Miss Antonia after she strained her throat with that song. Lemons this time of year."

Lee wiped off the counter. "Good thing Mr. John provides well for his family. Couldn't've bought a lemon otherwise."

Antonia. Antonia the atonal. Brigit drew in a quick breath. *Lord, that wasn't kind of me at all. I'm sorry.*

"Stop fussing like an old hen. You've gracious plenty on that tray for everyone to have the dessert of their choice now," Goodhew chided in an affectionate tone. "*They'll* all appreciate your food."

Goodhew said no more. As a butler, he embodied self-control and tact. Then again, he'd mastered the ability to speak great truths with nothing more than a silent twitch of his brow. Though Brigit had been in service here for a slim month, she knew the wry allusion he'd just uttered was out of character. The insult to his wife's cooking exceeded his tolerance; and though he'd served the young ladies with civility, his approval didn't lie with any of them.

I hope Miss Emily has someone better up her sleeve. Brigit pumped water into the sink. *Then again, for Duncan's sake, perhaps I should hope she doesn't.*

❧

"Taking some night air, Brigit?" Duncan smiled as he walked through the garden. With moonbeams catching wisps of her inky hair and making them go silver, it reminded him of a sprinkling of stars across a dark night sky. This woman made for a bonny sight.

"A fine night 'tis."

"Aye." He stopped by the bench she sat upon and lifted the book beside her. "Now what have we here?" He tilted it until the moon illuminated the spine, but the golden lettering didn't show up well enough for him to be sure of the title. A flick of his fingers opened the cover, and he read from the title page, "*The Pioneers*. So you found it."

"I did."

"I want to thank you for sparing my dignity this afternoon. No grown man wants to be caught escaping from his home because his sister is populating it with bridal prospects."

"'Tisn't any of my affair." She daintily folded her hands in her lap and looked at them. "You needn't say anything more."

"*Saying* wasn't the problem in the dining room; *whistling* was." His humor must have struck a note with her. She glanced up and smiled.

"Now that you're wise to Miss Emily's plans, I'm sure you'll either find she has a suitable bride among the lot she's chosen, or you'll manage to keep free from the parson's trap until you can shove off to sea again."

"No doubt, it's the latter. As I told you in the library, I'm not about to surrender to the war Emily is waging."

"Americans speak of war quite often."

"How long have you been here?"

She shrugged diffidently. "Long enough to know there's unrest in the nation, but there's serenity in the Newcomb home." A stricken expression crossed her face, and she popped to her feet. "Oh, I'm begging your pardon. I had no place, saying such a thing about your—"

"Think nothing of it." Duncan stayed where he stood, blocking her exit. "You complimented John and Emily. I happen to agree."

"Please excuse me." She took the book from him and scurried into the house.

Duncan watched her go. When he turned back, he spied her shawl. It had slipped off the bench and lay in a pool of—*cashmere?* He picked it up and fingered the fine fabric. What was a maid doing with such a pricey piece of goods?

"Duncan—I wondered where you went." Timothy strode toward him.

Duncan dropped the soft, pale yellow shawl on the bench. "Did you want me for something?"

"Yeah." A smirk tilted Tim's mouth. They fell in step and walked around a hedge, out of view from the house. Tim lowered his voice. "Mother is in rare form. She's bound and determined to stick you with a wife."

"So I noticed."

"Well, I thought you'd like to know she told Lily to gather flowers tomorrow morning so she and Anna could make arrangements for the parlor and dining room, and she asked Cook to make her Seafood Newburg."

Duncan stopped in his tracks. "Flowers are normal enough— but Seafood Newburg? Emily's escalating her schemes. Who's the next bridal prospect in her petticoat parade?"

"Opal Ferguson." Timothy toed a small rock. It skittered along and stopped at the edge of the path. "She seemed to have designs on Sean Kingsley, but he and Caroline eloped two weeks ago. Between Opal and her determined mama, you're going to be hard-pressed to slip out of the marriage noose."

Duncan groaned. "I thought we'd already scraped the bottom of the barrel. I've conversed with the abysmally mis-named Prudence. Adele actually drew a map in her mashed potatoes to demonstrate what portion of the States she estimates will revolt if Lincoln is elected. Antonia would break every glass in the house with that voice of hers. But Opal?" He grimaced. "I thought Emily loved me."

His nephew chortled. "She does. I overheard her telling Father a wife would settle you down."

"I'd sooner lash logs to a bathtub and row it across the Atlantic than be settled with Opal Ferguson."

"Opal generally gets whatever she wants." Tim shot him a pained look. "And she wants to be your wife."

"A spoiled henwit isn't to my liking. She cannot read or cipher any better than the twins. I'd never be able to go to sea and trust our home to her care."

His nephew poked him in the ribs. "You could take her to sea with you."

"I thought you felt a need to bite some salt air."

"Hey!" Tim gave him an outraged look. "Are you saying you won't take me if I don't help you evade the girls?"

"No, I'm saying nothing of the kind." Duncan wrapped his arm around his nephew and gave him a manly squeeze as he started to saunter along. "Though if I wed, according to family tradition, I'd be expected to take my bride on my next voyage—not my nephews. Any of Emily's prospects would cause me to jump overboard."

Timothy laughed.

"You, on the other hand—you'll be an asset. Aye, and I'm looking forward to having you help me teach some of the crew. The pity is, several of the immigrants who hire on can barely sign their names."

"I'd be glad to help, but I'm no schoolmaster or tutor, Duncan. I want to learn the ropes, just as you did."

Duncan stopped and gave the teen a solid pair of pats on his shoulder, then broke contact. "Ignorance lives in us all, Tim. It's just that we all have areas where we shine. A man's dignity is important. You'll trade them your book learning for their seafaring wisdom."

"Are you saying I'm going out this next voyage?"

"Emily will have her final say, but I'm planning on it—unless she shackles me with a bride." He twisted his features into an expression of distaste. "Sure as the sun rises, it won't be Opal. Once I heard Sean married, I feared I'd be her next target."

"Why is that? Because Opal's mama is so scheming?"

"I refuse to delude myself, Tim." Duncan stared out at the horizon from the hilltop of the estate. Moonlight danced on the waves until the ocean blended with the night sky. "I'm of marginal class. I'm a full-blooded Irish immigrant, and every last one of these lasses—especially Opal—would turn up her nose if I didn't have a ship to my name."

He paused, then continued. "I'm accepted in society because of John's marriage to my sister, and it's known I'll provide well for my bride; but truth is, I'll not be tied to a woman who believes she lowered herself when she wed me. If 'tis my family connections and money that draw her, 'twill be a miserable marriage."

"And you think I'll be any better off?" Tim jammed his fists in his pockets and paced back and forth. "My real father didn't even marry my mother—"

Duncan listened to his nephew. Tim rarely said a word about his birth, so he needed to blow off some steam. Taking him to sea would be wise. He'd always been a somber child, and his feelings ran deep. As he stretched into his manhood, he'd need self-confidence to counterbalance his true father's betrayal.

"It's proud of you, I am." Duncan stuck those words in before Tim could catch his breath and continue. Duncan had learned long ago that Tim rarely spoke his heart; and if he completely emptied it, he'd retreat in embarrassment. By listening to his nephew, then cutting the flow as it started to trickle down, Duncan knew he'd help the lad save face.

"Proud?" Tim gave him a stunned look.

"Aye. You're wise beyond your years. Many a man goes to his grave believing his worth was what others assigned to him. God gave His Son to ransom you—and that is your true value. Ne'er lose sight of that. Any man or woman who looks down on you isn't worthy of your love. John and Emily know that—and it's the secret of how they've made their marriage work."

"Then why is she trying to match you up with all these women? Can't she see how ridiculous it is?"

Duncan chuckled. "I wouldn't pretend to know the way my sister's mind works. The one thing I do know is, I'm grateful for your warning about tomorrow night. I'll sorely miss having Cook's Seafood Newburg, but 'tis a loss I'll gladly suffer since it'll allow me to avoid Opal and her mama."

Tim let out a sigh. "You wouldn't happen to include me in your plans so I could miss out, too, would you?"

A slow smile tugged at Duncan's lips. "It seems to me, I'll need some papers to show Old Kemper about the ship. Specifications. I'll leave them on the desk in my room. You might want to deliver them in the afternoon. Oh—and bring one more thing. It's very important."

"What?"

"Three licorice ropes."

four

Brigit sat by the window up in her bedroom. She could see Duncan and Timothy out on the lawn. Guilt speared through her. Rattled at how she'd babbled to Duncan instead of remembering her changed station in life, she'd scurried off.

It was truly Duncan's fault. The rascal could charm a river into running backward. She'd been minding her own business, enjoying the peaceful evening, when he happened by. He didn't have to stop. In fact, he shouldn't have. *But I could have stayed silent or excused myself straight away instead of sitting there, chattering like a magpie.*

She'd barely made it into the house when she realized she'd left her shawl on the bench. It couldn't stay out there—it was a special treasure. She'd gone back after it and overheard some of what Duncan said to Timothy.

Humility was a rare enough quality in men, but he'd taken it to an extreme. Why would a man like that feel he wasn't good enough for any woman in the town? With wonderful auburn curls and a ready smile, Duncan O'Brien looked handsome as Adam must have on the day of creation; and from his conversations, anyone could determine he was as smart as a whip. Aye, and generosity and patience also counted in his favor—she'd heard about his concern to teach his men to read. Yet Duncan didn't give himself credit for those fine points; he dismissed them and assumed the lasses wanted him only for the jingle in his pockets.

Granted, a sound marriage needed to be based on more than financial considerations—no man or woman wanted to be viewed only for the depth of their pockets—but to Brigit's way of thinking, Duncan underestimated his appeal. When

God made him, surely He'd made a good man.

Some lass would be blessed to have him. She heard Trudy bumping about in the room next door. Brigit let out a moan. The poor lass still carried a torch for Duncan O'Brien. A sad thing, that. Trudy built up her hopes each day, only to get them dashed when Duncan stayed oblivious to her presence. Miss Emily must have noticed the longing in Trudy's eyes because she'd been assigning her to tasks that kept her away from Duncan. For true, Duncan O'Brien deserved more than a mere servant as his bride.

❧

"Blest be the tie that binds—" Duncan suddenly stopped singing.

Prudence, dressed in yet another pink frock, twisted around and sang the next line of the hymn while batting her lashes at him. "Our hearts in Christian love. . ."

Trapped in church. Wasn't there something about amnesty— no, sanctuary—that's what it was. Church was supposed to be a safe place, a house of worship and peace—not a match-maker's hunting ground. The first hymn of the morning had been "How Shall the Young Secure Their Hearts?" which was followed immediately by "Love Divine, All Love Excelling." Now they were binding hearts in Christian love. *Lord, I'm sorry for the fact that I've ceased singing, but I'm sure You understand. I don't want to mislead anyone into thinking I'm planning a courtship. I'll just stay silent for this one hymn. . . .*

"How wonderful, knowing we are all bonded together in Christ's love." The parson beamed at the congregation. "Please turn in your hymnals to hymn number sixty-seven, 'O Happy Home, Where Thou Art Loved Most Dearly.'"

The pianist and organist both played the opening chords as Duncan glowered at Emily. A snicker sounded beside him, so he subtly stepped on Timothy's toes to hush him.

Lord, I'm a man of my word. I said I'd stand down for just that one hymn. Couldn't You have taken mercy and inspired the parson to choose a different hymn? Maybe "A Mighty Fortress" or "My Soul, Be on Thy Guard" or even "In the Hour of Trial"?

Duncan suppressed the sensation of being the center of attention and kept his gaze firmly on the cross at the front of the sanctuary. He took a deep breath and started to sing with the congregation. "O happy home, where Thou art loved most dearly. . . ."

five

"Psst. Unca Duncan. C'mere."

Duncan spied his youngest nephew on the far side of the umbrella stand. It provided barely enough cover for the lad; Duncan wouldn't stand a chance of remaining unseen.

If Emily doesn't leave me alone, I'm going to start living aboard a landlocked ship or convince John to start sending me on the transatlantic voyages so I can get away from this never-ending petticoat parade.

Phillip pressed a forefinger to his lips and used the thumb on his other hand to point toward the dining room. In what Duncan supposed was intended to be a whisper, the boy announced, "Girls."

Duncan didn't need to be told. The cloying scents of several floral fragrances mingled and gave warning. He glanced toward the stairs, pointed upward, and reached out for Phillip's hand. Gleefully, Phillip launched from his hiding place. He snatched Duncan's hand, and they hastened for safety. They reached the first step, and Duncan let out a sigh of relief.

"Duncan!" Emily's cheerful voice stopped him dead in his tracks.

Phillip let out a loud groan. Duncan wished he could do the same. Instead he glanced over his shoulder. "Hello, Emily."

"I was rather hoping you'd be home for lunch. Please come join us. Phillip, did you wash your hands?"

"Yes, Mama." Phillip turned loose of Duncan's hand and wiggled his stubby fingers in the air. "See?"

"Good for you. Now go get your brothers." She gave him a Mama's-wise-to-you look. "I expect all three of my sons to be at the table immediately. Be sure to tell them Uncle Duncan is joining us."

"Yes, Mama." Phillip scrambled up the stairs.

Emily approached. Duncan couldn't decide whether to growl or smile at her. The words were on the tip of his tongue to tell his sister to stop this stream of marriageable material—he simply wasn't fishing. Then again, manners demanded he not embarrass her. The time would come for him to confront her when these young ladies were gone. In the meantime, at least he'd have his nephews with him, so he could steer the conversation to include them and bore the women to tears.

"Several young ladies are here to visit Anna Kathleen and Lily."

"Is that so?" The ruse was so painfully thin, he felt a stab of disbelief. *Does Emily think I'm so stupid I wouldn't see past that lie?* Then another thought crossed his mind. If these scheming minxes were using his nieces as a means of getting to him, he'd put a stop to it here and now. He refused to allow his family to be used as tools.

Emily had threaded her arm through his and started toward the dining room. She must have felt his sudden tension, but she didn't stop. Lips barely moving, she said, "I need you to display your best manners. You're an example for my children, you know."

A stream of giggles filled the air.

Duncan groaned and shot his sister a heated look.

"You can make it through this. I'll help you." A charming smile lit her face.

How many times had Emily said that to him? She'd been true to her word each and every time. Long ago, when he'd been but six slim years, she'd taught him how to change Timothy's nappies. She'd held him close at their sister's grave-side and made the same promise. Aye, and when they'd both needed to learn the finer points of gracious living after she wed John, she'd been his confidant and ally. They'd literally gone from rags to riches, but no matter what her circumstances, Emily was Emily. He loved his big sister for that.

"I'll do this for you." He gave her a tender smile.

"Thank you."

Duncan mentally battened down his hatches for the storm ahead. He'd weather it. 'Twas but one insignificant meal. Aye, and with his nieces and nephews at the table, he'd most certainly find a way to enjoy the luncheon. A single step more, and he could see the staff had added every last spare leaf to the dining table, elongating it to accommodate twenty. Twenty!

"How long have you been planning this little event?"

"Since Sunday," Emily admitted in a gratingly cheerful tone. They walked into the dining room, and she singsonged, "Look who's joining us!"

Anna Kathleen twirled about. Her hoops swayed precariously; but rather than making her usual sound of exasperation, she beckoned. "Duncan! How wonderful! Do come meet my friends."

Duncan glanced about. A solid dozen or more young girls filled the room. Frilly party attire in nearly every pastel hue turned the room into a veritable feminine rainbow, and most of the girls were still young enough to wear their hair down. Relief coursed through his veins. He'd not been duped into a matchmaking scheme—these lasses still spent their days in the schoolroom.

Lunch passed with relative ease. Duncan found the youngsters refreshing. When Timothy shot him a stricken look, Duncan determined the brunette in the greenish dress seemed to be far more interested than his nephew wished. Recalling the youngster on Tim's other side was named Bernice, Duncan smoothly went to the rescue. "Tim, have you told Miss Bernice about your plans for next month?"

The brunette clouded over, but Tim and Bernice both lit up. Tim shot Duncan a grateful look, then focused his attention on the red-haired girl. "I'm to help with the fittings on my uncle's new vessel, and I'll be going on the next voyage to Massachusetts."

Duncan congratulated himself. All went well enough. Since it was an unscheduled event in the middle of a busy day, he didn't mind the fact that he'd need to rearrange some of his plans. Family came first. Being the wonderful mother she was, Emily had concocted this little affair for her daughters and sons to enjoy their friends and learn the necessary social skills to help them through life. Duncan figured the least he could do was serve as an example.

Or so he thought until a flock of mamas and big sisters swept in to collect the girls.

Pink Prudence, Adele, and Antonia—whose name he'd not recall unless he associated her with a similar sounding name, A-Tune-ia—all made appearances. Oh, and he'd been introduced to a few oh-so-available sisters who were home from finishing school as well as the gangly, bucktoothed granddaughter of their nearest neighbor. Decorum demanded he act with utter gentility. Under any other circumstances, he'd not mind a bit. This rated as different, though. Duncan felt like a sailor who fell overboard into a school of hungry sharks.

Tonight he would sit Emily down and make it plain. No more of this nonsense.

❧

Brigit sat in the nursery with the twins. She'd come up to mind them so Mr. and Mrs. Newcomb could have a quiet evening together. The little girls filled the last ten minutes with complaints, bemoaning the tragic fact that they hadn't been included in today's party. Left over little treats from the luncheon party remained in the kitchen, so Brigit suggested,

"June and Julie, why don't we have our verra own bedtime tea party?"

In no time at all, the three of them huddled at a small table. They weren't alone. Three tin soldiers stood at attention on the empty side of the table. "Now aren't you clever lasses?" Brigit nodded approvingly. "We've handsome companions for our party, and I doubt anyone ever saw such a scrumptious spread."

"I'd have to agree," a deep voice said from the doorway.

Startled, Brigit twisted in her chair to see if her ears had deceived her. No, they hadn't. Duncan O'Brien lounged against the door frame, arms folded, his hair wind ruffled, and a twinkle in his eyes. He tilted his head to the side, and a rakish smile lifted the right side of his mouth.

"Do you want some tea, Uncle Duncan?"

Before Brigit could object, he pushed away from the door and started toward them. "Of course I do. I'm so thirsty, I could drink the ocean dry!"

June went into peals of laughter; Julie giggled and managed to spill tea onto the saucer.

Duncan towered over the children's table, and Brigit wished he'd just bend down, gulp the tea, and depart. He didn't cooperate. No, he didn't. Instead he picked up each soldier, precisely set one to the left of each of them, then scanned the room. Who would have ever imagined what he did next? The big, handsome, ship's captain swept a china doll from a bed. He pulled out the last little chair and folded his tall frame onto it. He sat the doll on his knee and surveyed the table.

"You've gathered a fine spread here. Shall I ask a blessing?"

The girls folded their hands and pretended not to peek. Brigit compressed her lips to keep from smiling at the fact that she and Duncan were doing the selfsame thing. He said a short, sweet prayer, and they all chimed in, "Amen."

"Are you hungry?" June started pushing tiny plates at him.

"Ferociously hungry, and so is my little cousin, aren't you, Fortuna?" He toggled the doll and raised his voice into a falsetto. "Why, yes, I am."

"Fortuna?" Julie scrunched her face.

"Oh, haven't you ever met my cousin? How remiss of me. June, Julie, and Miss Brigit, allow me to present my cousin, Miss Hunter. Miss Fortuna Hunter."

six

Brigit choked on her tea. She managed to murmur a greeting to the doll and watched Duncan waggle his brows. "I was sure you must have met her. All of her friends were here today to pick up their little sisters. She told me to be sure to have some cake."

"June, serve Mr. O'Brien—"

"Duncan," he interrupted.

Brigit nodded acknowledgment. "—Duncan some cake."

June leaned forward, then halted. "Do I have to use a fork?"

"If you use your fingers, I'll have to lick them clean."

Never had a tea party been so charming. Brigit delighted in watching how Duncan played with his little nieces. He unabashedly enjoyed them. Someday he'd make a wondrous father.

Miss Emily bustled into the room. Brigit suddenly sobered. *What am I doing?*

"I thought I heard merriment in here. Duncan, John wanted to speak with you about something."

"Mama, we're having a tea party!"

Emily petted her daughters' curls. "I can see, darlings."

"Tea and treats before bed," Duncan said as he rose. "I'm sure you'll have sweet dreams." He kissed June and Julie, then left the room.

Suddenly the whole room seemed far bigger and dreadfully empty. Brigit quickly picked up the mess and crumbs, placed everything on a tray, and dampened the end of a towel so she could wash up the twins.

"So you enjoyed your party?" Miss Emily asked as she helped her daughters into their flower-sprigged flannel nightgowns.

"Uh-huh." The twins answered in unison.

Brigit started to comb Julie's hair so she could plait it for the night. "They have very nice manners, Miss Emily."

"As do you." Miss Emily smiled easily. "You've said little about your family, but I'm guessing you're more accustomed to directing staff than being a member of one."

Her words made Brigit draw in a quick breath. "I'm sorry, Ma'am. I—"

"No, no. You misunderstand me. We'll talk later."

Later. The taste of the much-too-sweet tea and treats suddenly came back and switched to bitter, and Brigit swallowed hard. *Lord, You know I need this job. Aye, You do. Whate'er I've done wrong, help me. My parents need the money I make, and if—*

"Ouchie!" Julie reached up and grabbed the base of her braid. "You're pulling too tight!"

"I'm sorry." Brigit loosened the weave a tad and deftly tied the tail of the plait with a bit of ribbon.

"She complains of that almost every night," Miss Emily said as she tied June's matching braid. "When you girls go to school next year, Julie's going to scream half the time when the boy behind her tugs on her pigtails or dips them in the ink well."

"I won't let them do that to her." June's outraged words rang with certainty.

Emily laughed. "You might be too busy taking care of yourself to guard her."

June and Julie scrambled into the bed and snuggled together. Brigit picked up the tray as Miss Emily bent over to kiss her daughters. "Let's say our prayers."

"We already said prayers with Brigit and Uncle Duncan."

"You can't pray too much."

Brigit headed down the stair, dread in her heart. In the slim month she'd been here, she'd seen Miss Emily shelter her children. The easy laughter in the nursery didn't mean all was well—it merely showed a mother's regard for her children's innocence. *Whatever she wants to talk to me about, it's surely not going to be a good thing.*

Miss Emily's words echoed in her mind. *You can't pray too much.*

❧

John wanted to give Duncan a receipt for a special order he had waiting in Massachusetts. The postal delivery brought the letter to the dock today, saying the ring for Emily was ready to be picked up. As brothers-in-law went, Duncan knew he'd been blessed with the best God ever made. Each year John made it a point to give Emily an anniversary surprise. For their upcoming fifteenth anniversary, he'd commissioned a diamond and sapphire ring.

If Emily caught wind of it, she'd cancel the order and spend the money on charity. John donated generously to any number of causes, but Emily always managed to ferret out some family in need. John had learned to dodge Emily's openhandedness by sneaking around and evading her questions. When he managed to give her the gifts, she was always so touched that she cherished whatever it was. . .and John would simply assure her she could name whichever needy situation she knew and he'd give twice as much to it.

Diamond and sapphire. Duncan saw a sketch of it. Emily was still a simple woman at heart, and she'd not want anything ostentatious. John and the jeweler traded letters until the design reflected the perfect style. Duncan hid the slip of paper in his Bible, knowing full well he'd be sure to take it with him on his next voyage.

He'd come out of his bedchamber as Brigit carried a tray down the stairs. Now there was a fine lass. Her startling eyes matched the blue dress she wore, and it seemed a smile never left her lips. He'd stood in the doorway, watching how she sat at that little tea table with his nieces. Not a one of the young women in Emily's Bridal Brigade would have ever set up such an enchanting party for two little children and join in as she did. The few minutes he watched her, he'd been impressed by the way she gently took the opportunity to reinforce basic decorum and yet encouraged the girls to use their imaginations and pretend.

How had she known June and Julie felt left out today? Duncan remembered being that young. His sisters were so much older; and once Emily was to wed John, Duncan felt that he didn't exactly belong in their world. He wouldn't admit it to a soul—it would have sounded baby-ish—yet John understood. Just before the wedding, John took Duncan aside and gave him a shiny, new Seated Liberty quarter. He'd told Duncan he was a worthy part of the family—a full quarter of it. John, Emily, Duncan, and Timothy—there were four of them, all starting a new life together. If ever he felt he didn't belong or wasn't wanted, John ordered Duncan to pull that special quarter from his pocket and rub it. He'd not needed to. The quarter itself served as such a potent reminder that Duncan counted it as his greatest earthly treasure. He watched Brigit disappear behind the kitchen door and jingled the coins in his pocket. She'd understand. Aye, a woman like that who bothered to make children happy would. And it made her a treasure in her own right.

❧

Later. Later turned out to be a mere half hour after they tucked the twins into bed. Miss Emily passed by Brigit and murmured, "Come to the kitchen."

Too nervous to do much of anything, Brigit sat at the kitchen table and kept her hands knotted in her lap. Miss

Emily set the creamer on the kitchen table next to the simple earthenware teapot and started to stir her cup. "The day I hired you, your speech and mannerisms told me you'd not grown up in a humble village cottage. Plain as could be, you'd known what it was to have a fine education and social exposure. Oddly, though, your hands weren't the soft, smooth ones of a person of leisure."

Since the lady of the house posed no direct question, Brigit held her silence.

"Each time I've an opening, I ask the dear Lord to bring the right lass to that position. He gave me that sense of rightness about you, Brigit Murphy. I hired you on, but I didn't pry one bit. No, I didn't—but I am now." Miss Emily took a sip of her tea, then softly urged, "Tell me how you came to be here."

" 'Tis the same story I'm sure you've heard many times over by now. The blight struck, and the famine grew worse."

"But your family owned the land; they didn't till it."

Brigit nodded.

Miss Emily reached across the table and pushed Brigit's cup and saucer closer. "If a sip of tea cannot soothe you, you're surely not Irish. Drink up, Lass."

The sip of tea did give comfort. Brigit smiled.

"I live in a fancy home, Brigit, but 'twasn't always the case—and, sure as the sun rises, you've heard that fact. Fortunes can change just as fast as a tide. 'Tisn't the surroundings that define who we are; 'tis our hearts."

Which is why she's so comfortable sharing tea with me in a humble kitchen instead of her fancy parlor.

"So let the tea loosen your tongue," Miss Emily said, "and share your heart with me."

Brigit traced the edge of the saucer with her fingertip to delay answering the personal invitation. "Mum always said there wasn't such a thing as too much tea, but I doubt she'd shared a children's tea party ere she made that pronouncement over her next cup."

"Where's your family now?"

"Mum and Da live in town." She lifted her cup and half-whispered, "On Willow Glenn." Naming the street that teemed with tenements left a sour taste in her mouth so she took a hasty sip.

A beauteous smile brightened Miss Emily's face. "So you're not here alone. Have you any brothers or sisters?"

"Nay—just the three of us, there are." Though Miss Emily treated her with great warmth and Christian kindness, Brigit tried not to pour out all her private business. This woman wasn't her friend; she was her employer. "God be praised, we all stayed together."

"Do your parents have enough to eat?"

The tea nearly sloshed over the brim in Brigit's cup. "That they do, Ma'am, and I thank you kindly for asking."

"Before I met my husband, about all I could buy was milk; and even then I had to water it down. We near starved."

"So that's why Duncan likes milk now."

Miss Emily gave her a slow smile. "Aye, and it's sweet you are to understand that fact."

Miss Emily asked several leading questions, then finally poured herself a second cup of tea and let out a satisfied sigh. "I can see my faith in the dear Lord wasn't misplaced. Truly, you're an answer to prayer." Miss Emily asked Brigit to take on the duty of working with Anna Kathleen and Lily on social skills—conversational abilities, personal grooming, and curbing their hoydenish tendencies.

"Anyone could see you possess the refinement to handle those matters, Brigit, and the responsibility also carries with it an increase in wages." The grandfather clock chimed from deep within the house. "Now then, since we've settled things, I'm supposing we ought to turn in for the night."

Brigit rinsed out the cups and pot, then barely slept that night because she lay in bed praising the Lord for His generosity and goodness.

❧

"Bad pennies always turn up."

"I beg your pardon?" Brigit stopped dusting the dainty porcelain statue of a shepherdess on the hallway table. With no one else around, she thought Duncan had addressed his words to her.

He cleared his throat. "I—um—I was trying to recall the old saying, 'Bad pennies always turn up.' What of the good pennies?"

She shrugged. "Mayhap some kind soul spent those in a charitable way."

"Could be." He walked off, muttering to himself.

Pennies. Brigit smiled to herself. She'd been waiting for Duncan to leave so she could go clean his chamber. Last night, Miss Emily assigned her the responsibility of regularly tidying his chamber. Nothing specific was said, but Brigit gathered Miss Emily had caught wind of Trudy's infatuation and wisely chose to place distance between Duncan and the giddy maid.

The sheets smelled like fresh air. The scent filled the room as Brigit snapped the sheet to unfold across Duncan's bared mattress. She smoothed it, tucked in the corners, and swiftly added the top sheet and covers. Crisp cases on the pillows, curtains drawn open, and water exchanged from his washbowl, and she'd gotten a fine start on her chores for the day.

Arms full of sheets, she headed into the hallway and ran smack into Duncan. "Oh, I beg your pardon, Sir."

He braced her elbows and frowned. "Aren't you working awfully hard?"

Brigit wrinkled her nose. "Not at all. Sprucing up a home is a constant thing, but Miss Emily is diligent to keep matters well in hand. Besides, Mum always said hard work ne'er hurt a body."

"Hmpf."

"If you'll excuse me, Sir—"

He turned loose of her and peered over her shoulder into his room. "Are you done now?"

"Not quite. I'm to salt-sweep the carpeting; but if you'd rather, I can come back after I've done a few other chores."

Duncan pushed past her and scowled at the beautiful green-and-gold Turkish carpeting in his room. "It looks perfectly fine. There's no need for you to tend the flooring."

What man worried over the details of housekeeping? Baffled and also torn by allegiance to Miss Emily, Brigit moistened her lips and murmured, "I'll check with the mistress."

"I'll talk with Emily. If you wait a moment, I'll give you something to place in Timothy's room. He asked to study star navigation, and I have a few charts. . . ."

Mindful of propriety, Brigit stayed outside the chamber as Duncan went in. She watched Duncan cross the room with his self-assured stride. He stopped at his desk and reached for the key in the lock, then froze.

Duncan turned around. "There were tiny golden hearts dangling from this key."

"Perhaps they fell off."

He stepped back so he could survey the carpeting. His scowl evaporated. He stooped and grabbed what looked to be short, thin red cords with a trio of hearts. "Here we are."

"Now aren't those pretty wee things!"

"Aye, and I'm glad they're not lost. Many a year ago they belonged to my sister Anna—God rest her soul. Em and I plan to give them to her namesake someday. In the meantime, I'm to keep them out of sight. Last night I decided since little Anna Kathleen wouldn't be in my chamber, I could put them on my keys and enjoy them myself for a time."

"I'm sorry you lost your sister."

"Did I hear my name?" Miss Emily came down the hall.

"Aye." Duncan grinned at his sister. "Anna's three golden hearts fell off the key, but they're found."

"Good!" Miss Emily beamed. "Timothy said you'd promised him navigational star charts. I thought to take them to the library instead of his room. Titus is curious, but he'll crumple the edges. Best we think to unfurl them on a table downstairs."

"Fine." Duncan lifted his chin in an unconsciously imperious move. "Brigit, I'll take the charts below. You may leave."

❧

Duncan waited until the maid was out of earshot, then gave Emily a thunderous look. "Do you need more funds to run the household?"

"Why, no. John is quite generous. What makes you ask such a thing?"

"You're working Brigit too hard."

Emily gave him a withering look. "Now, our Duncan—"

"Don't you 'Now' me. That lass is underfoot no matter where I go. She said you'd ordered her to salt-sweep my carpeting."

"I did."

"It doesn't need it!"

Emily smiled at him in her I'll-be-patient-with-you way. "I won't let things get filthy ere I see to them. Maintaining a smooth home means doing things on a routine. 'Tis time for your carpeting to be either beaten or swept. The salt will brighten the colors, but if you'd rather have all the furniture moved so Brigit can beat—"

"No. Absolutely not."

Emily hitched her shoulder. "Then 'twill be salt-swept."

"Then don't have her change linens and dust, too." To escape Emily's calculating look, Duncan turned to rummage through his desk. "I may have been but a scrap of a lad, but I remember all too well how exhausted you were from cleaning before John brought us here. I thought you'd kept sensitive to not overworking anyone else as you'd been."

"Has Brigit said anything to you? Complained—"

"Not a word," he interrupted. "It's just that everywhere I go, she's right under my nose. I don't see you working any of the other maids that much."

"Brigit is well educated. The children love her, and I have her work with them more as a result."

"That might account for a portion—but not enough."

Emily let out a choppy sigh. "Very well. I'm keeping Trudy and Lee working together. Trudy's developed an infatuation for you, so I took pity on you and—"

Duncan lifted his hand. "Enough said. After she leapt into my arms from the stairs, I've taken to avoiding her like the plague. And since we're on the subject, Em, I insist you cease playing Cupid. I won't stand for it."

"We've always been a social family. I'm not about to stop having people over because you're marriage-shy."

"You're not just having 'people' over; you're bringing in eligible women. I'm not fooled for a minute."

"The women's circle sews together every other Tuesday."

He snorted. "What about that gaggle you had in last week?"

Emily gave him an exasperated look. "If you had any manners, you wouldn't refer to that. MayEllen Reece is in confinement, and we all wanted to celebrate the coming little blessing."

"I might grant you that one, but every other day you have a lass here for a meal. Em, don't prevaricate. It's as if you toss out birdseed and every last goose and henwit in the county takes a turn pecking at our table."

She muffled a sound he couldn't quite interpret. To be sure, she looked displeased. "I have the perfect name for your vessel. Based on the way you're acting, it should be called the *Recalcitrant*."

"I'm not recalcitrant; I'm independent. *When* I determine I'm ready to wed, I'll do my own choosing. I'll court a woman with common sense and a kind heart. Until then, Em, cut it out."

"There's nothing in the world wrong with my letting you have a look at who's out there."

"You're wasting your energy. By the time I'm ready to wed, every last one of these lasses will be married and have a babe or two." He gave his sister a hug, then decided he'd made his point and it wouldn't hurt to praise her a little. "I know your motive is good. I'm thankful you have a happy marriage, and it's endearing to know you want the same for me. When I'm ready, I promise, you'll be the first to meet my girl."

Emily beamed up at him. She stood on tiptoe and patted his cheek. Duncan felt a spurt of relief. He'd finally gotten through to her. He smiled.

"Duncan, boy-o. You're in the right of it. I *will* be the first to meet your girl. That's why I'll have to introduce the two of you!" Emily twisted from his hold and hummed as she walked away.

It wasn't until she started down the stairs that Duncan identified the tune: "The Time I've Lost in Wooing."

Late that night, when Duncan climbed into bed, he caught himself ironing his hand over the crisp sheet. He pulled his hand back and growled under his breath. That pretty Irish maid with the beguiling blue eyes had changed this linen and smoothed it in place so nary a wrinkle marred the surface. She'd plumped his pillow, too. He took it, turned it over, and thumped it for no reason whatsoever.

No matter where he turned, there were women. He'd grown accustomed to living at sea, being surrounded by men. Even in the close quarters of a ship, men understood how their crewmates needed solitude and space. Here on land where room abounded, women clumped together and clucked over every little thing. It could drive a man daft.

The last thing Duncan wanted was to come into his chamber and have thoughts of that maid, Brigit, haunt him. Her quick wit, bright eyes, and attention to detail left her all too perceptive—not that he had anything to hide; but she'd been here, fussing at Emily's insistence. She'd straightened his things, dusted his bookshelves, and even left the faintest hint of citrus behind. Was it lemon and beeswax polish, or did she wear lemon verbena?

That did it. He was an orderly man. He kept his cabin on his vessel clean, and he could jolly well make his bed at home. He'd tell Emily not to have Brigit in here again.

seven

"So that's how it's to be for now."

Brigit bit her lip and nodded.

"There now," Miss Emily crooned. "Duncan's in a foul mood, and 'tisn't your doing. 'Tis mine, truth be told. Aye, that it is. I've crowded a few too many lasses about him, and he's needing his chamber to be a refuge."

"Yes, Ma'am."

"Your position is safe here, Brigit. I'm delighted with you. So let's discuss your duties for today."

Brigit listened and diligently carried out each assigned task. The Newcombs ran an odd home—the help worked only a half day on Sundays, and they each had another day off during the week. In addition, each of them also had one evening off on a weekly basis. Tonight she'd go visit Da and Mum. That thought warmed her as she collected the laundry and delivered it to the laundress.

When she entered through the kitchen, Cook flashed her a smile. "I just took inventory of the pantry, and I'm needing to rearrange things. A handful of girls are due in tomorrow to help me with canning. Have the other maids told you about this?"

"No. I'm willing to help. I'm not precisely sure what to do with those orange things, though."

"Pumpkins." Cook smiled at her. "They make a wondrous custard or pie." She flapped her hand back and forth. "But that's neither here nor there at this moment. I'm going to have Trudy and Lee wash out jars for me. Goodhew put crates in the pantry, and you'll go help me sort through the jars."

"What are the crates for?"

"Why, Miss Emily sends a crate of jars to the staff's families along with flour, sugar, and such so they'll have the essentials for holiday baking. It's a household tradition. She does it once a season—autumn, Christmas, Easter, and summer."

Brigit stared at Cook in astonishment.

Cook tugged her into the spacious pantry and whispered, "Miss Emily was practically starved to death when Mr. John found her. She'd given her portion of food to Duncan and their sister Anna. Anna—bless her soul—made it through birthing Timothy, but she was just too weak. The very first thing Miss Emily did as mistress of Newcomb House was to come into this pantry and make boxes for the maids' families. Now where shall we begin?"

Brigit looked around at the countless tins, sacks, barrels, and jars. Shelves, cupboards, and bins filled the large, square room. Canned apricots sat at eye level on the nearest shelf. "Oh, Mum loves apricots," she blurted out.

Cook laughed. "Then help yourself. While you're at it, put a pair of jars in the next crate for my sister."

"Glory be," Brigit said slowly. "The dear Lord's in heaven, and He's reaching down to provide for us."

❧

He had no one to blame but himself. He'd taken Emily to task for overworking Brigit, so now Emily had the maid taking the girls to Newcomb Shipping's warehouse for an afternoon of hunting through the bolts of fabric. They were to select flannels for the women's sewing circle to make blankets and nightgowns for the local orphanage.

The girls would be underfoot at the house with the autumn canning, so the excursion made perfect sense. All in all, the plan should work out beautifully—except for the fact that John had an appointment, so Em decided Duncan could drop them off on his way to the dock and pick them up later.

So here he had June standing between his legs as he drove the carriage, and Brigit sat beside him with Julie on her lap. Anna Kathleen and Lily took up the other seat, much to his relief. Until they were seated and others were out of range, his nieces practically killed anyone who ventured close with their parasols. He'd have to talk to Em about teaching the girls to handle those dumb things better, else they'd blind someone.

As the carriage rolled down the main tree-lined street in town, another carriage stopped alongside his. Opal and her mother were riding along with Prudence and another woman. He couldn't very well ignore them, so he tipped his hat.

June asked loudly, "Uncle Duncan, which one of them is Fortune Hunter?"

The outraged expressions and sounds coming from that conveyance made it clear all of the women heard June's question.

"June, the name is Fortuna, Darling." Brigit's words rang out. "Fortuna was an imaginary name for the dolly. It means to be blessed or lucky. We all need to look for the blessings in our lives."

Grateful for Brigit's quick thinking and diplomatic solution to the sticky situation, Duncan nodded, then smiled at June. "And you want to be a blessing to others."

"Is that why we're getting 'terial for the orphan babies?"

"Yes," he answered.

"'Tuna Hunter didn't get a blessing," Julie pouted. "She got lost. I can't find her."

Anna Kathleen called over, "You all are welcome to join us if you'd like!"

Duncan bit back a groan. If the ladies accepted Anna's invitation, there was no way he could leave society ladies in the warehouse. He'd be obliged to go along and endure them all afternoon. Brigit had enough common sense to mind the girls and keep them together with her. She'd capably select practical fabrics with a minimum of fuss or bother. Compassion had filled her eyes when she'd been told of the purpose of this outing, and Duncan knew beyond a shadow of a doubt that the only material she'd want would be for the motherless children. He'd be able to assign a man to push along a cart for Brigit and assure their safety, then leave and tend his own business.

On the other hand, visions of Prudence pulling out yards of pink satin or Opal heading toward the brocades made Duncan's hair stand on end.

He strove to school his expression. "Someday we'll have to plan some other kind of outing, Anna. The ladies are wearing such fetching dresses, they'd never want to get them soiled in a musty old warehouse."

"Yes, well, we will be coming to the ladies' sewing circle next Tuesday," Opal singsonged as she ran her fingertips along a ribbon in her day gown. "You girls go on ahead. Be sure to pick out some lovely little pieces so we can brighten the days of those unfortunate waifs."

Prudence leaned forward. "I'd be happy to help today."

Opal's mother cut in. "Pru, Dear, your mama would swoon if I took you home with cobwebs and dust all over that rose taffeta."

"Another time. Good day, ladies." Duncan drove off and didn't even try to smother his smile. Pink had some use after all.

eight

"Details. They're just minor details," one of the carpenters grumbled as he tromped off with a toolbox.

Duncan held his tongue. It wouldn't serve any purpose to bark at the men. The frustrations he faced were myriad; yet none of them would be lessened by snapping at someone. His ship still needed appreciable fitting before it would be seaworthy and capable of handling a fully laden hull. After listening to the discussions around him, Duncan felt more pressured to hasten the maiden voyage.

Hotheaded men already scrapped with one another about politics, and everyone had an opinion about the Lincoln-Douglas debates. Whichever leaning they held, those men weren't above trying to convince others to see matters in the "right" way. He had his hands full keeping the workmen on task and off the political bandwagons. More often than not, Duncan found it necessary to stop a scuffle between his workers because some staunchly advocated secession while others firmly believed in preserving the Union. All he needed was for someone to get upset and sabotage the vessel. Once it was launched, he would have far better control over who came near it.

Newcomb Shipping boasted fine crews of seamen, and there'd never been anything but cooperation at sea. Discipline was both rare and fair. Some of these hotheaded men could tear apart the crew's harmony. Duncan made mental notes of the few who were rabble-rousers and also of those who were peacemakers.

Duncan wasn't a man to vote by party recommendation— he studied the candidates, prayed, and finally came to the decision he felt was best. The word "secession" came up often, and folks were hot under the collar. He wished the Lord's peace would be poured out on the nation.

"Duncan, I'm needing more timber," Old Kemper called from several yards away.

"Fine. I'll have a draft ready for you at the office. When do you want it?"

Kemper sorrowfully shook his head from side to side and swaggered up. "Nay, that's not the issue. 'Tis that the mill's behind on deliveries."

"Then we'll send wagons for whatever you need. Probably ought to lay by some extra if they're running late on our orders."

"I was hopin' you'd say that. Can't take my men, though. I need every last man jack. You'll have to pull some deckhands. Sooner you do it, the better off we are." Kemper brushed some sawdust off the front of his shirt. "I'm already looking at a delay because of this."

After arranging for a team of sailors, Duncan sent them off with him to get the lumber. He went to examine the sails on another vessel and dickered with a supplier over the rising cost of tar.

Every last contact contained some reference to the election. Duncan didn't want to engage in political conversations. He tried to sidestep them as best he could. Folks lost all reason when they found someone didn't share their leanings. Duncan planned on casting his vote in the privacy of the ballot box and prayed whatever the outcome, his loved ones would be spared any of the discord's ravages.

John met his gaze and subtly tilted his head toward the shipping office. He rarely sought a meeting in private. Most of their discussions took place out in the shipyard or on the docks. The fact that John indicated he'd rather handle a matter out of sight let Duncan know it must be important.

Duncan cupped his hands to his mouth to create a bullhorn. "John—I need to get some papers signed. Can you meet me in the office?"

His brother-in-law nodded.

Duncan hadn't lied. He did need John's signature on a few things. Those matters were resolved in minutes. Unfortunately, folks kept coming in and out. John grimaced. "Let's have a quiet supper tonight. I'll instruct Emily that she and the children can eat early. Hey—have you seen my fountain pen?"

"No. Why?"

John shook his head as he rummaged on the top of his desk. "I can't find it at home and wondered if I accidentally carried it here or if you'd borrowed it by chance."

"Sorry. Haven't seen it."

John heaved a sigh. "It'll turn up. As to the other matter— we'll dine in the library at seven, if you're free."

"Done." Duncan figured John had plenty on his mind. They'd both been busier than a one-armed man in a rowboat. 'Twas time to compare notes.

&

"I'm needing butter." Brigit surveyed the cart and determined what else would complete the meal.

"Here you go." Lee plunked down a small dish.

"I'll be happy to wheel that on in." Trudy bustled over and curled her hands around the handle of the ornately inlaid wooden cart.

"I imagine you would, but you're not going to." Cook used her ample hip to bump Trudy away. "'Tis dishes for you tonight. Get with it, now."

Trudy let out a gust of a sigh and pouted. "I don't know why I can't take the tray in to the gentlemen. I've been here longer than Brigit."

Brigit didn't want to be party to this conversation. She

popped the domed covers over the plates to hold in the heat and filled the creamer.

Cook didn't mince words. "You're not assigned that task, and for good cause. You make a pest of yourself every time you get in the same room as Duncan."

"I do not!"

"And just who dropped beets on his arm yesterday?"

Trudy looked completely affronted. "That was an accident."

"I've never seen anyone so accident prone," Lee added in a wry tone. "The way you tripped on the stairs and he had to catch you—"

"Oh, stop! Mishaps occur to everyone." Trudy pressed her hand to her bosom. "No one can begin to imagine how mortified I was to tumble down the stairs in front of him."

Lee snapped a dish towel at her. "For it being such an embarrassing calamity, Goodhew said you sure did manage to cling to Duncan for a long while."

"I could have broken my neck. He rescued me, and I was suffering a reaction."

Cook folded her arms across her chest and narrowed her eyes. "Tripping down one measly step wouldn't break your neck. It's a crying pity you didn't thump your noggin and knock some sense into yourself. Any other lady of the home would dismiss you for the way you're literally throwing yourself at a family member. 'Tis unseemly. Stop whining and do your job, and be glad you've kept it thus far."

Brigit turned the cart around and bumped the swinging door with her hip to open it. She backed out of the kitchen and drew the cart after her until the door shut. Once out, she seesawed the cart back and forth at an angle until she had it turned around. The library lay just a few doors down the hall.

Goodhew waited until she brought the cart to the door, then opened it and announced, "Dinner, sirs."

"Yes. Good." Mr. John's voice drifted out of the room along

with the pleasant scent of the fire Brigit had lit in the room an hour before.

She pulled in the cart, and the door shut behind her. Mr. John sat behind his desk, and Duncan stood by the fireplace. Brigit got no cue as to their desire, so she asked, "Will you gentlemen be dining off the cart, or would you prefer to use the desk or one of the tables?"

"That table there will do just fine." Mr. John gestured toward a table flanked by a pair of deep green leather wingback chairs. He then turned his attention back on Duncan. "It's not a matter of greed. Emily suffered from such poverty. I'll never have her in a position where she needs to worry again."

"And you have my undying gratitude for that." Duncan grabbed an andiron and poked at a log. The logs let off a cheery popping sound, and sparks flew.

Brigit quietly spread a small, plain white linen cloth across the table, then set the plates down and laid silverware beside them. She took pains to make as little noise as possible. The somber tone of voice the men shared brought forth memories of when Da and Mum were discussing the grave matters of sending the farmers to America so they wouldn't starve. Tears misted her eyes.

She poured coffee for Mr. John and placed the glass of milk for Duncan next to the other plate. Once everything was in place, she pushed the cart off to the corner, came back, and removed the warming domes. "Supper is served."

The men took seats, and Duncan asked a blessing. Brigit waited until he finished before she set the domes on the cart. It would have been disrespectful to make that racket while he'd been addressing the Almighty.

"We need to set up priorities at once," Mr. John said. "Plan. I'll hire some men to do patrols on the grounds."

"Thank you for the milk, Brigit." Duncan took his glass.

Mr. John continued. "I expect our vessels to be conscripted right away. Supplies are of the utmost—"

Duncan lifted his chin at a self-assured angle and spoke in an uncustomarily sharp tone, "We'll have Goodhew summon you if we need anything, Brigit."

"Very well."

She gladly left the library. Whatever the two men were discussing, it should be between only them. The very fact that they were holding this private meeting underscored the importance of discretion, and Brigit felt horribly intrusive, standing there. Servants were supposed to be invisible and silent—but she'd been out of place when the men so obviously wished to hash out this business.

"Back so soon?" Trudy simpered once Brigit reached the kitchen. "Don't you know to stay and clear away? Men don't take long to eat."

Jealousy dripped off each word, and Brigit decided to put Trudy's fear to rest. "That may be, but Duncan dismissed me. I'll just have to go back later."

Later. Hopefully much later—after the men had finished and left the library. Brigit felt completely unsettled. Memories flooded back of so many evenings of similar conversations filled with concerns and burdens her parents held. *Lord, whatever is weighing on the hearts of those men, please help them carry the load.*

※

"It's heating up and will hit boiling point all too soon." Duncan set down his fork. "I'm striving to stay impartial in public."

John nodded. "There comes a point when a man has to stand up and be counted. When the time arrives, we'll not be silent. Until then, we have to set priorities and keep as neutral as possible."

"I'm thinking of protection."

"As am I." John took a gulp of coffee and grimaced. "Cook must've measured the coffee wrong. This stuff is so weak, it needs crutches. Why did you have that maid leave?"

Because she looked worried and pale. Brigit's normally been bright as a copper penny, but she wasn't tonight. Pushing that cart in here, she was the cheerful-hearted lass I've become accustomed to seeing; but within seconds she changed. She's perceptive, and she sensed the ugliness of what we're discussing. She gave us a trapped look, and tears filled her eyes—I wanted to spare the lass. It all sounded so melodramatic. Duncan hitched a shoulder. "We have no reason to think she's untrustworthy. I prefer to have no one privy to our conversation, though." He paused, then tacked on, "Women ought not be burdened with such dark matters anyway."

"True enough. So as for protection—I want to purchase guns. Several of them."

"And you don't think that will raise suspicions?"

John grinned. "It's customary to give gifts at the boat's christening. We can order a goodly number of navy Colts and present them to Old Kemper and several of the other men. No one is going to keep a precise count, so we'll be able to keep a reasonable stash here."

"What about Timothy and Titus learning some marksmanship?" Duncan chuckled at the memory of the horrendous fuss his sister kicked up the first time she learned John had taken him out to do some target practice. "Do you think Em will allow it?"

"While you were away on your last voyage, I went down to the caretaker's cottage to talk to your father. He and I have been working on Emily a bit at a time—dropping hints so she could grow accustomed to the notion. At first she pitched a fit, but she's had a chance to let the idea sink in."

"I could tell her a Colt is more manageable and accurate for the boys. Safer by far, too." A distinct memory of that first time he'd fired John's rifle flitted through Duncan's mind, and he winced at it. "The kick from a rifle would knock them over."

"Your father sneaked Tim off a few weeks ago and let him discover that fact firsthand." John unconsciously rubbed his right collarbone. "I smuggled Tim some liniment that night to lessen the bruise, but he sported an impressive one."

"Gunpowder and bullets—what is your plan about those?"

The men talked long into the night—making plans and setting priorities. If war didn't occur, they'd easily use all the supplies in the course of time. If matters continued down the road of doom Duncan predicted, they'd need every last bit.

Aye, that was the sickening part of it all. The United States looked as if they weren't long to remain united. In a war, the North and the South would surely inflict wounds that would be slow to heal. With Virginia counting itself as the South and participating in the Southern economy, it would be doubly difficult since the capitol was right there. This region would be in the middle of the skirmishes.

In the event of a war, Newcomb Shipping would be an immediate target for the factions. Each side would want to lay claim to the vessels. The very thought that the vessels they used only for peace would be conscripted for war left both men cold. By loading half the ships and setting up long-term voyages and trade agreements, John planned to keep a good part of the fleet out of the fray. His strategy ought to work well enough to keep them from being party to a good portion of the predicted violence.

John drummed his fingers on the table. "How do you stand, if it comes to fighting?"

nine

Duncan stared him directly in the eye. "I'm not eager to take a life; but if it comes to the point that we go to war, I'd represent our family. I want you to stay out of the fray. Em and the children need you too much." Duncan didn't want John to give him any grief over that assertion, so he smoothly changed the direction of the conversation. "Have you thought about what you want to do with the family? Will you keep them here since we were discussing firearms earlier?"

John shook his head. "It's one of the reasons I'm sending the boys with you to Massachusetts on this next voyage. It'll give you a good reason to drop in on my aunt. Discuss the matter with her. If she's amenable, I'll have Emily and the children stay with her for a season or two until the danger passes."

"You think Em will go for that?"

"She'll battle me." John wiped his mouth. "But Em loves the children, and in the end that will tip the balance in my favor. She'd do whatever is necessary to keep them safe."

Duncan absently swirled his glass until the milk turned into a whirlpool. "No matter whether you have a Northern or a Southern sympathizer, everyone is sure that if it comes to a battle, the whole matter will be over in a few months."

"We can only pray if it comes to that point, they're right. Now let's determine what supplies to stock up on and how to go about it."

Plans. They made their plans in seclusion over a fine meal and by a warm fire. Detail after detail needed consideration. The very next morning both men started to carry them out. Within days Duncan was glad they'd buckled down right away. Events around him made it abundantly clear they had assessed the political situation all too accurately. The nation was teetering on the precipice of civil unrest.

"Hey—did you read the article in *The Spectator* about Yancey's speech?" the sail maker asked as Duncan inspected the cloth he proposed to use. "It says here, 'As a declaimer and specious reasoner, he has few superiors. As an ingenious debater, seeking to place fairly and frankly before the country a faithful record of facts and an incontrovertible accumulation of unimpeachable testimony, he was, in his effort of Wednesday, totally and painfully deficient.'"

"Hmm." Duncan tested the thickness of the fabric and frowned.

"Are you unhappy with the editor's opinion or with my goods?"

"I was considering having you make an extra set of sails to keep on hand. The last storm cost us dearly, and 'twould be wise for me to place an order." Duncan rapped his knuckles against the cutting table. "You can deliver them as you make them."

"Yes, I believe I could work in your order."

"Fine. Draw up the order and have the papers delivered. John or I will sign them and send a deposit. John may wish to order additional single sails or cloth. Be sure to include pricing."

The sail maker couldn't hide his greedy smile. "Of course. Of course. I'll be right on that."

"Excellent." Duncan made a speedy exit and silently congratulated himself. He'd managed to tend to yet another of the priorities he and John agreed upon. If, indeed, war came, Newcomb Shipping needed to be wholly independent. Even if it meant sending some of the ships off on extended voyages to safeguard their fleet, they'd be able to do so if he and John continued to split these meetings and make acquisitions without raising any suspicions.

If anything, the fact that his own vessel was in the works made it that much easier. Each time he placed an order, merchants presumed he was fussing over his "baby." He could, in all honesty, confess that to be true. He did attend to each and every last detail. 'Twas no lie, and he held no shame for that fact. A ship carried souls across the unforgiving ocean; and the least little mishap, miscalculation, or mistake could be disastrous. He freely said as much, too. Everyone promptly agreed—some out of wisdom, others out of greed. Nonetheless, it allowed him to place an order for half again as much lumber because he'd nearly run out, for twice as much hemp rope, and a full ton of iron for his blacksmith to make fittings.

&

The next day Duncan came down to breakfast and was asked to drop Emily and the children off at the shore. John and Emily decided since the weather was turning and today looked to be fair, the children would do well to have a nice outing. Though John said nothing, Duncan fully understood his motive. If things settled down after the election, the children's trip to the shore was still a fun time; if politics got ugly and the Newcombs decided to take the children away, they'd have a fond memory.

Emily left the breakfast table claiming she wasn't feeling well. Before she left, Emily asked Brigit to fill in and supervise the outing. According to plan, Duncan would leave her and the children at the shore, where they'd hunt for shells and enjoy a picnic. He'd simply pick them up a few hours later, after he conferred about his new vessel and booked cargo for the upcoming voyage.

Seven children, a dog, a blanket, art supplies, and a picnic basket took up the entire back of the wagon. Brigit turned three shades of pink when Duncan said she'd have to ride up on the bench seat with him. That very fact charmed him—it also made him decide he'd not allow her to trade places with

Anna Kathleen, as she started to suggest. She might well be in charge of the children, but he was in charge of the outing.

"You're a quiet one," he said after they'd traveled down the road a ways and she'd not said a single word.

She shot him a nervous smile. "It's kind of you to drive us to the beach."

He tilted back his head and chortled. "Brigit, you might think I'm the worst kind of cad by the time I come to reclaim you. I'm stranding you with a wild tribe."

"But the day is lovely. We've sun to keep us warm, plenty of room to romp, and enough food to feed the town."

Once he selected a spot and stopped the wagon, Duncan hopped down, then reached up to assist Brigit. His hands spanned her tiny waist quite easily. Once more he appreciated how gracefully she moved. She thanked him prettily, and yet again he noticed her speech and conduct seemed far too refined for a simple housemaid. If Emily wouldn't make rash assumptions, he'd ask her about Brigit's family and background. As it was, he didn't dare. Satisfying that idle flash of curiosity would tilt Emily back into her matchmaking mode.

"Titus, you carry the blanket," Brigit said as she took visual inventory of the supplies. "Timothy, you're the strongest. I'll ask ye to carry the picnic hamper. Lily, be a dear and carry the wee crate with our paints and such. Yes, there you have it. Phillip, I'm trusting you to keep hold of Barkie's leash. Anna Kathleen—the twins will be yours and mine. I fear 'twill take the both of us to keep them in line."

Duncan stood back and watched. Brigit organized the children in short order. Instead of running off willy-nilly, they'd listened and obeyed. He helped settle them, then promised to return later.

Timothy and Titus swam like fish. So did Barkie. Duncan barely reached the shipyard ere he realized he'd not ascertained whether Brigit could. Not a one of the girls could swim a stroke, and Phillip wasn't any more accomplished than they. He should have given stern warning to the children that they weren't to get wet. What if one of them got overeager, went out, and—

John slapped him on the shoulder, jarring him from his concerns. "Wait until you see your cabin. The fittings are in."

"Yes. Um, John—can Brigit swim?"

John nodded. "Em asked her."

"Good. Good." But what use was the skill when Brigit's skirt used a full five yards and she undoubtedly wore the customary three layers of petticoats beneath that? Sodden skirts like that would work like an anchor.

"Franklin arranged for an entire load of cotton for Massachusetts, and the *Cormorant* is ready to set sail, but Josiah's taken ill."

Duncan glanced over at the vessel and nodded. "I can make the run."

"I hoped you'd volunteer. The delivery's set for the Boott Mills in Lowell." John batted away a pesky gnat. "I've talked Em into letting you take Timothy and Titus along on the next voyage—but this trip is unscheduled. If you'd rather pass or handle just one of the boys, I'll certainly understand."

"It's good news all around. My cabin's together, Franklin closed a deal and saved us time, and the boys are to get their feet wet." Duncan shook back a stubborn, curly lock of hair that the wind kept flinging down his forehead. "It's no trouble for me to take both. Tim might have wanted to be alone for his first voyage, but I'm thinking Titus will keep him good company."

John squinted at the rigging of a nearby vessel. "Aye, there's that."

Duncan dropped his tone. "And they need to meet relatives up North. If your plan becomes necessary, they'll do better if they're familiar with the new surroundings."

"Go on—see your vessel, and pick up the children afterward."

Worry lined John's face. "Wind's taking on a bite to it, and I don't want them catching whatever Emily's come down with."

※

"Brigit, I need to pack the boys' bags for their voyage."

Brigit stood up so quickly, she banged her shoulder on the banister she'd been polishing. "When?"

"Now. Duncan just told me the captain of the *Cormorant* is sick, so he's taking the helm. The boys will be going with him. Have Trudy and Fiona finish polishing the wood, and you come help me."

"Yes, Ma'am." Brigit washed her hands and passed on Miss Emily's instructions to the other maids, then went upstairs to join her. She found Miss Emily standing by the wardrobe in the boys' room. She had one hand braced against it for support. Brigit hurried to her side. "Miss Emily, you're white as a cloud. We'd best tuck you in bed straight away."

"I'll lie on one of the beds and supervise; you can put everything in their valises. The laundry's fresh and ready so you can pack it now, and the boys can wear what they have on today when they board in the morning."

"Sure as can be, God must be smiling down on this plan for all to be ready like that."

Miss Emily settled onto the mattress and gave her a weak smile. "I like the way you think, Lassie."

"Why don't I borrow a blanket off this other bed—"

"Stop fussing. We have work enough to do." Miss Emily closed her eyes and started to list the items they would need. "Two good shirts for when they're in Massachusetts. Two of the old ones to wear at sea. . ."

As Brigit carefully folded each garment and layered them into the boys' bags, she decided not to trouble Miss Emily with the details. A quick look through drawers and the wardrobe provided most of what they needed, and the rest of their necessities lay on the washstand.

Emily wiggled on the bed and let out a resigned little sound. "Poor John and Duncan. Most men are tense, what with worrying about the future of our nation. Feelings run high about such matters. John says he hopes once the election is over, things will settle down."

"That would be a pure blessing indeed."

"Brigit, I hope for miracles from God, not from man. John and Duncan are up to too much at the shipyard and spending too much time talking to each other in low tones."

"Is that what's wrong? Have you been worrying yourself sick?"

"What turns my stomach is, Newcomb ships have always been used for peaceful commerce. Even when others transported slaves, the Newcombs refused to make money in such a dreadful manner. John and Duncan fear that if war comes, the ships will be conscripted and fitted with cannons."

Brigit shook her head as she latched the valises. "There's a sorrowful thought."

"Duncan's been cantankerous as a shark with a toothache, but it's my fault for making this trip home so miserable for him. He's normally quite charming, and I hoped to help him settle down. You might have noticed I invited a few young ladies over."

Brigit compressed her lips to keep from laughing at that understatement.

"It seems I didn't spark a match; I sparked his temper."

"I'm sure it's not just that one thing." Brigit tried to watch her words. "Your brother must know you love him very much."

Emily sat up and grasped the covers on either side of her hips. "Ohhh."

Brigit reached out and steadied her. "Perhaps you ought to lie back down."

Rubbing her fingertips across her much-too-pale forehead,

Miss Emily said in a faint tone, "I planned to handle preparing Duncan's things myself. I don't think I'd better. Please, will you do me the favor of packing for him?"

"Of course I will." Brigit took Miss Emily's arm. Miss Emily steered them into Duncan's chamber and promptly melted onto his bed.

"Be sure to include that new shirt I had you sew." Miss Emily yawned. "He'll need everything you put in for the boys, and he'll also need his lucky coin."

❧

How in the world is a man to keep his sanity? Duncan headed down the companionway to his cabin. Two days at sea. It felt like an eternity, and he could hold the weather only partially to blame. It used to be he couldn't wait to set sail again. He'd no more than dock, and he'd be itching to cast off again. He liked the jig and reel world of his rowdy crew and the brotherhood of the sea. So why did he want to be on land?

Emily's matchmaking schemes would have made a lesser man break out in hives. I ought to be glad I escaped. Aye, I should— but I'm not. And it's all that blue-eyed maid's fault. The realization made his mood grow even more foul than the weather had been.

Duncan shut the door to his cabin and trudged toward his bunk. Salt chafed his skin, and wherever salt didn't, damp clothing did. As far as voyages went, this one rated as downright miserable thus far. They set sail and started out with fair weather and good hopes. By midafternoon a squall blew in and battered the *Cormorant*.

Timothy had been horrendously seasick. Even now, he lay on Duncan's bed and looked downright puny. The lad's face still carried a sickly tinge of green. Titus, on the other hand, sat in the center of a hammock they'd suspended across the cabin. He rocked it like a swing and whispered, "He's still sleeping."

"You ought to be, too. I have plans for you in the morning, so you'd best rest up." Duncan waited until his nephew plopped down and was nearly swallowed up in the hammock. He let out a sigh of relief as he shed his clothes, sponged down, and put on a dry outfit. His stomach rumbled.

"I'm hungry, too." Titus popped back up. "I know how to get to the galley."

"I'll bet you do; but aboard a vessel, men don't pilfer the way you sometimes did when you wandered into the pantry and kitchen at home. That kind of undisciplined access to the provender could leave us all stranded and starving."

"Oh." Titus waited a beat. "You're the captain. You can do whatever you want."

Duncan hung his wet clothing up on pegs and slipped a thin strip of twine across them so they'd not sway free and plop on the deck. He scowled at a pile of fabric in the corner. "What is that mess?"

"Huh? Oh. My clothes."

Duncan crossed the cabin in a few long strides and unceremoniously dumped his nephew out of the hammock and onto the deck. "Aboard a vessel nothing is left out. It shifts and slides, and a man can trip as a result. There's no maid here to baby you. You'll be a man and clean up after yourself."

"Yes, Sir."

Duncan left the cabin. When he returned, Titus's clothes occupied pegs and were secured with twine. "Well done. Come share a bite with me. Afterward I'll dump you into the bunk with Tim and take the hammock. I'm warning you now, I'm going to snore enough wind to send us clear to Massachusetts by morn."

Titus muffled his chuckle and scrambled to the captain's desk. They shared a hunk of cheese, some soda bread, and a pair of apples. "Uncle Duncan, do you think Mama misses us?"

"Emily is bound to miss you. Me? She's used to me coming

and going." Brigit's image flashed through his mind. He suppressed it at once and cast a look over at Tim. "Has he kept anything down at all?"

"Lemon drops." Titus pulled out a small tin and rattled it. "Brigit gave them to us. She said it would settle a tipsy stomach, and it did."

The mention of that maid he'd just thought of only served to sour Duncan's mood. Women. God created them for His purposes, and Duncan acknowledged that. He even granted they made the world a far better place—but only from a distance. Marriage? That lay several years in the future. *Then what am I doing, thinking of Brigit and marriage at the same time?*

Duncan cleared his throat. He didn't want to grouse at his nephew any more than he already had. "Enough. You go climb in with Tim. I'm manning the hammock."

Weary as could be, Duncan barely managed to finish thanking the Lord for pulling his vessel through bad weather and watching over his family before he mumbled amen and fell asleep. He didn't dream one bit; but when he opened his eyes, he had a strange sense of having traveled back in time. Years ago he'd awakened in a hammock in this selfsame cabin when he accompanied John on voyages. The memory was a fine way to start the day.

Duncan spotted the valise he'd secured on a peg next to the wardrobe when he boarded back home. It would take a few minutes to unpack, so he started in.

Emily always insisted on packing for him. The way she didn't fuss yet showed her love in countless ways warmed his heart. When he married, he wanted a good woman like Em—one whose capabilities and caring would make for a happy home.

Each article of freshly starched and pressed clothing fit in his compact wardrobe. A new shirt appeared—a fine one at that—not a fancy one for Sunday best, but one that featured full-cut shoulders and plenty of sleeve to allow ease of motion while on board.

He'd felt oddly bereft the past few days, realizing he'd left something important ashore. Duncan knew he couldn't very well order the ship back to port to allow him to run home and get his special quarter, but its absence left him uneasy. . .until he felt something in the fabric of the new shirt—his quarter! *God bless Em for seeing to that detail.*

He treasured that assurance and always kept the coin with him on his voyages—a touchstone that reminded him he had a home and loved ones awaiting his return. He curled his hand around it and glanced at Tim and Titus. *I'll bring them back to you, Em. You can count on it.*

ten

The Cormorant docked in Lowell, Massachusetts. Duncan made sure all was well and gave orders for the southern cotton to be delivered to the Boott Mills. He traced his finger down the register. "See here, Tim? The agreement is for the entire cargo. Every last bale, each of them approximately one hundred pounds. The mills run by water power, but the water level there is low, so the bales will travel by barge."

"Do you have to arrange for the barges?"

"Your father or Franklin already tended to that matter. Because we do this run so regularly, Newcomb Shipping is able to book for the services."

"Uncle Duncan, can't you take something home that's better than dumb old material?" Titus wrinkled his sunburnt nose. "We already have millions and millions of bolts in the warehouse."

Duncan shook his head and ignored the exaggeration. "A deal was struck. A man sticks to his word. We've lined up buyers for the fabric. Already most of it is earmarked for Europe. It'll go out the week after Christmas."

"On your new ship?"

"Aye," Duncan said, stretching the single syllable into a long, satisfied sound. "'Tis to be my new home at sea. For now, though, we need to pay our respects to your aunt."

After his nephews were settled in with Aunt Mildred, Duncan went back to the docks. The lads needed to stretch their legs, and their aunt had plans to keep them busy. Especially if they would have to come live here, they'd need to forge a comfortable relationship; and Duncan didn't want to run interference. Business wasn't just a necessary obligation; it also supplied a reasonable excuse for him to take his leave.

The next three days, bales of cotton left the holds of the *Cormorant* and rode the barges to the mills. The space vacated filled with bolts upon bolts of cloth. Brightly printed calicos, practical shirting, and sheeting accounted for the greatest portion of the order. Duncan did spot-checks of the loads to assure the quality didn't waver. He also made a trip to the warehouse and selected a variety of the finest Lowell had to offer. Those bolts were muslin wrapped and stored with additional care.

The bustle and rhythm of commerce appealed to Duncan. He thought to take Tim and Titus with him for a day as he tended to business, but he dismissed that plan immediately. Almost to the man, each contact slid into some political discourse.

Duncan had hoped the rhetoric wouldn't be so strident since they were so far north. Though he privately agreed Lincoln would be a godsend as the president and didn't support disunion, he also understood some of the economic issues driving the unrest in the South. He personally believed all men were created equal—that his Irish roots didn't make him any less God's child; so why would African roots make a man less worthy of respect or God's grace? The hopes he'd held that Lincoln might heal the rifts evaporated as rapidly as the steam that powered the looms in the mills.

After the ship's hold filled with the goods and they were set to sail with the tide the next evening, Duncan sat down to supper with Aunt Mildred and the boys. He rather hoped if he broached a certain subject, Aunt Mildred would volunteer to assist him. "Emily wanted me to buy some prints for the staff."

"Prints?" Aunt Mildred's eyes widened. "Now that's different."

"Mama doesn't like to do things the usual way," Titus said. He took a gulp of potatoes.

"She's a very uncommon woman," Aunt Mildred agreed. Her voice held no censure. Indeed, Duncan recalled she'd been infinitely kind to Em when John wed her and she needed to learn the ways of society. "I confess, I like the blue she's used for your household staff. Black is so dreary."

Duncan leaned forward. "Come along and help me make appropriate selections. You'd have a better notion of what Em would like."

"I have every confidence you'll do fine. I already promised Tim and Titus I'd take them to the museum."

Duncan nodded. He couldn't begrudge the boys a nice outing.

Timothy started to chuckle. Duncan shot him a questioning look, and the chuckle turned into a full-throated chortle. "Buy pink. Nothing but pink. I'll bet Prudence Carston suddenly stops wearing it if you do, because she'd never want anyone to think she's an ordinary woman instead of one of society's darlings."

Pink. The next day after he picked up the ring John ordered, Duncan stood in the warehouse and stared at the fabrics. He glanced at the pinks and winced. *How did I let Em saddle me with such a ridiculous errand? As often as she goes to the shipping office and rides by the warehouses, she could have gone in and chosen whatever suited her fancy.* Duncan gave fleeting thought to pleading that he was simply too busy, and it would have been the utter truth; but the special quarter in his pocket reminded him of how family cared for one another. He'd do this for Emily.

Em wanted prints. She'd also specified they were to be pretty and of good quality. He'd handled cloth aplenty, and judging quality presented no problem. The real problem lay with selecting something reasonable. Pretty prints abounded—many made with the newest aniline dyes so they had eye-catching color. He wanted to make this a quick grab-and-dash type of task; but to his consternation, he couldn't.

"As you can see, they're arranged on the shelves by color." The warehouseman waved his arm in a wide arc to encompass a veritable rainbow. "The blacks and browns are practical. Keep the dirt and wear from showing."

Duncan headed toward the grays.

"Those are especially suitable for second-year mourning attire."

Disenchanted with that bit of information, Duncan turned toward the blues. Blue. The color of Brigit's extraordinary eyes. No, he refused to be beguiled by her. Besides, Em was tired of blue.

"Greens are favored this year." The warehouseman leaned against the cart he'd pushed along.

Greens looked fresh. Appealing. They'd set off Brigit's hair and—Duncan cut off that line of thought. Yellows would show every last smudge. As often as she—no, all the maids—he corrected himself—dusted, the gown would look filthy.

Ah. Respite. White. Duncan felt a wee bit of the tension drain away. He'd been wanting to buy some white for himself. Aye, he did. When he got home, he'd get Emily to tell him who sewed that new shirt. She'd placed the order so she'd be able to direct him. He'd never had a better fit—the generous cut across the shoulders didn't bind, and the extra length made sure it stayed tucked in. He'll supply more cotton and place an order for her to make him a good half dozen more. He'd make sure, though, that he'd simply handle the transaction in writing. Knowing Emily, she hired some comely seamstress in hopes that he'd fall in love. He'd rather swim to England than deal with his sister's ridiculous, romantic machinations.

A single bolt—that was all he'd need. Straight off the loom, a bolt held sixty yards. The printed cloth was processed and cut into half that length. Duncan squinted and noticed the bolts of white had also been halved. He shrugged. Thirty yards would keep him in shirts—what about John and the boys? Titus and Tim both washed their shirts aboard the ship and nearly tore them to shreds. They were growing fast. Duncan chose two bolts of white. White. Aprons. Emily always had the staff wear them. Brigit had a charming habit of slipping her hand into her apron pocket and tilting her head to starboard just a bit—a telling cue that she was thinking something through. He chucked a third bolt onto the cart.

"I thought you said you were wanting colored prints."

The voice behind Duncan pulled him from his thoughts. He stared at the cart and couldn't believe what he'd done. *Ninety yards. I just grabbed ninety yards of white.*

"Don't mistake me. You chose the finest white we carry. Mayhap I misunderstood—"

"No, not at all. I also want prints." Duncan strode ahead to the next set of shelves. Pink? He shuddered. The shade of Prudence.

Only women of ill repute wore red.

He turned the corner and gave up on trying to reason through what choices to make. Duncan impatiently grabbed several bolts and heaved them onto the cart. Even then Duncan kept picturing how Brigit would look dressed in almost every swath of cloth he touched. Brigit. Aye, she was quite the lass. Pure of heart, quick of mind, and kind in spirit. A rare woman indeed.

Duncan halted dead in his tracks and marveled under his breath, "Well, blow me down. I was so set on swimming free of Em's marriage net that I jumped right out of the water and into the boat."

"What was that?"

"Show me your bridal material."

eleven

Home. While at sea, Duncan felt the ocean was his home; but when he landed and rode up the drive to the Newcomb estate, his heart filled with an unmistakable warmth that told him he belonged here. He cast a glance over at Tim and Titus. Clearly they felt that same tug. They unconsciously kneed their mounts, and all three of them galloped the last mile.

"Why are there so many carriages and ribbons?" asked Titus.

"Can't you remember anything?" Timothy gave his brother a scathing look. "It's Phillip's birthday. I'll bet that's why Duncan got so pushy about us setting sail."

"I wasn't pushy. I was emphatic. A captain sets his timetable, and the crew needs to adhere to it. Discipline and control are essential on any vessel."

"Yeah, well, those are all right, I suppose." Titus wrinkled his nose. "I just didn't like some of the other rules."

Duncan gave him a long look. "No more shedding your clothes like a snake. That voyage trained you to be a man. Now act like one."

"I'll make you proud." Titus stared back at him. "You have my word of honor."

His word of honor. Duncan nodded. Honor. Integrity mattered to him above all but God and family. The one thing he couldn't abide was dishonesty or deception. He couldn't very well come home and pretend indifference to the woman he loved.

What would he do about Brigit, now that he'd returned? In the time he'd been gone, he'd reconsidered the whole situation and come to the same conclusion over and over again:

He loved her. She'd been in his thoughts nearly every waking minute, and he'd dreamed of her, too. She read well and enjoyed the same books he did, could carry on an intelligent conversation, and showed devotion to his family. Aye, she was a sweet woman.

Marriage to her wouldn't be a trap; it would be a joy. He'd need to court her a bit. Women put store in such customs. If he had his way, he'd just stand up in church Sunday and let the parson help them speak their vows. The first step would be making sure the feelings were mutual; then he'd do the right thing—go to her parents as well as settle her in with his own folks down at the caretaker's cottage. That way he'd see her every day while the women took care of the social details of arranging the wedding. It shouldn't take long. After all, he'd already seen to getting the fabric for her bridal gown.

Brigit. There she was, standing on the veranda, holding hands with June and Julie. The cashmere shawl about her shoulders drew Duncan's attention. He wanted to use it to tug her into his arms for a welcome-home hug and kiss, but he'd not do such a thing.

"We're home!" Titus shouted.

"We've been waiting!" Julie and June shouted back. Both tried to tug forward, but Brigit held them back. A wise move, that. If they were to shriek or move rapidly, they might startle one of the boys' horses.

Brigit didn't meet Duncan's gaze. Instead she smiled at Timothy and Titus. "We're looking forward to hearing all about your grand adventure as sailors."

"Tim got seasick the first day," Titus blabbed.

"Titus was homesick the whole time," Tim shot back.

The girls both giggled at their brothers' rivalry, but Brigit squeezed the twins' hands. "Now will you be taking a chance to fill your eyes with the sight before you? Your brothers left as lads, but I'm sure as can be they've come back men now. Taller and smarter, too."

"What about Uncle Duncan?" Julie asked.

"Your uncle." Brigit stretched out the words to allow herself time to respond. Duncan wondered how she'd get herself out of this. He didn't have to wait a second more. "Your uncle was already tall and smart before he left."

"Let me tell you how smart," Tim chimed in. "Wait until you hear about when we were at the—"

"We can all wait," Duncan cut in. Brigit rated as one of the most clever women he'd ever met. She weighed her words carefully around the children, and that discretion rated as a fine quality indeed.

"It won't take me long to tell the story—" Tim protested.

" 'Tis Phillip's birthday." Duncan put the slightest bit of pressure on his horse's side to keep him from dancing and bumping hindquarters with Tim's mount. "We need to go stable these mounts so we can celebrate Phillip's special accomplishment, too."

"What 'complishment?" June asked.

"He got older." Duncan nodded his head to give weight to his ridiculous comment. "It won't be many years ere he's taking to sea, too."

☙

Brigit wanted to go hide in the kitchen and help Cook. One look at Duncan let her know she hadn't been exaggerating how handsome he was when she thought of him. He looked so manly, with his brown, caped greatcoat flying behind him as he'd ridden up, and his roguish smile and deep voice gave her the shivers. She might very well make a fool of herself if she didn't mind her actions. The last thing she wanted was to lose her job because she flirted with a member of the family she was supposed to be serving. *I thought Trudy acted like a lovesick puppy, and here I am, twice as bad.*

She and the twins were supposed to greet the birthday party guests, so she'd been out on the veranda, planning on welcoming a dozen or more rowdy little boys. Brigit had seen a trio on horses in the distance and expected they were more guests. She'd felt her heart lurch when she recognized who the handsome young man was, riding between the two youngsters. Duncan had come back.

Brigit promised herself she'd keep her distance from Duncan. What with all the guests, that ought to be an easy thing to do. She figured the last of the guests must have arrived, so she went back inside with the twins.

Miss Emily believed in simple, honest fun. Instead of setting up several parlor games, she'd specified that Phillip's guests were to come in warm play clothes. With everyone assembled, she turned them loose in the back. Soon they were making snowmen and sledding down the hill.

The maids and the stablemen stayed out on the lawn, overseeing the children's safety. Brigit soon gathered up some of the children and lined them up to join her in a game of tug-o-war. Duncan didn't stay in the house with the adults; he'd come outside, too. Phillip shouted with glee, and Duncan eyed the rope and the boys.

"I want to be on your team," Phillip said.

Duncan strode over and had his nephew flex his biceps. He tested the little arms and nodded. "You're stronger. I think you and your friends should pull against me." He looked at Brigit and added, "And her. Just the two of us against all of you mighty little men. What say you?"

"Aye!" Phillip hadn't answered alone. His friends all chimed in with him.

As they prepared to tug, Brigit stood in front of Duncan and warned, "You made a bad decision. You won't be getting much from a weakling like me."

"You'll put your heart into it. That'll make us winners."

He turned out to be right on the first match. On the second, Brigit couldn't dig her heels into the earth well enough. Her boots slid, and her back knocked Duncan down, and she fell over him—or had he let go and caught her so she wouldn't fall? She couldn't tell. The very thought that he'd be so chivalrous made her heart patter. She scrambled to her feet.

Duncan rose. "Are you all right?"

"Fine."

Many of the little boys gravitated toward the strapping man, much to Brigit's relief. It let her scoot farther away. In no time at all, "Captain Duncan" had the "crew" of youngsters making forts from hay bales and ice blocks. It made for a glorious mess.

"Brigit!"

She turned when he called her name. White exploded all around her. Duncan stuck his hands in his coat pockets, looked up at the sky, and started to whistle as if he were innocent as a babe.

"Unca Duncan got you!" Phillip shouted from inside the snow fort. "He made a snowball by chipping an ice block."

"That was a sneaky thing to do," Brigit protested.

"You know what else is sneaky?" Phillip grinned at her. "He made me one for my birthday!" Phillip threw that snowball at her, but it fell short.

"I'm needing soldiers and warriors," Brigit called out. "Duncan O'Brien just declared war, and Phillip is in his camp. Who's going to stand by me?"

"We can play Capture the Flag!" someone shouted.

In no time at all, an epic "battle" ensued. In the midst of it, Duncan charged across the yard, vaulted over Brigit's melting fort, and tossed her over his brawny shoulder. He plowed through the broken-down bales of hay and headed back to his side. "I've got the princess! I captured her. We win!"

The children went wild, and the adults cheered.

Breathless—more from his contact than from being carried over his shoulder—Brigit couldn't say a word. He
stopped and set her down next to his team's fort. Standing
like Colossus with his hands on his hips, he asked loudly, "So
what say you now, my raven-haired maiden?"

*Oh! I'd have been just as happy for him to carry me away. If I
stand here, I'm going to make a fool of myself. I can't let him know
I have tender feelings for him.* "I'm not a flag!"

"But you're holding your team's," he pointed out. "And I
got you."

Brigit grabbed the scrap of red cloth someone draped over
Duncan's fort. "But you let go, and I have your flag now! You
counted your chickens a minute too soon."

He looked at her and nodded slowly. "We both did."

"We did?" She sucked in a sharp breath and squealed as a
chunk of ice slithered across the back of her neck.

Duncan swept both flags from her hands and chortled.
"Well done, Phillip."

Several of the children cheered and clung to Duncan, and
his laughter rang out. The man loved children. Aye, and they
adored him back.

Even after the party ended and the house quieted down,
Duncan sat on the floor and voiced his admiration for the
gifts Phillip received. Brigit gladly finished picking up the
last of the mess and hastened out of Duncan's presence. He'd
kept slanting her glances she couldn't interpret. *Lord, I don't
understand why he's giving me those looks. Has he guessed that I
hold feelings for him? What am I to do?*

twelve

The first rays of sun shimmered on the dewy lawn. Brigit looked out her window and touched the ice cold pane. Another day. "Lord, be with me today. Keep me strong and give me wisdom to behave as Your daughter."

After washing up, Brigit donned one of her blue wool gowns and brushed her hair until it crackled. Her fingers fumbled with the hairpins as she recalled what Duncan called her yesterday. *My raven-haired maiden.*

The man was a rascal. That he was. He'd acted like an overgrown boy. She refused to give him another thought. All it did was rob her of her peace and sanity. Brigit savagely stabbed one last pin in place. On days like this, she reconsidered her opinion of Miss Emily's no-cap policy. Wearing a cap might well have merit. In fact, Brigit thought she'd vote for a complete night-styled mob cap if given the chance. Wouldn't that be just perfect? Then Duncan couldn't say a thing about her hair. He'd never see it.

She dropped her buttonhook and had to get down on her hands and knees to fish it out from beneath her bed. After she used it to fasten her ankle boots, Brigit frowned at the bed. She'd mussed up the counterpane. That wouldn't do. No matter that another soul wouldn't know. She'd know, and that was reason enough to flick it back into order. Miss Emily provided individual rooms for the maids, and the appointments in them far exceeded what a girl in service might ever dream.

Aye, and I'll be in service until I'm no longer a raven-haired girl, but a gray-haired old woman, she thought as she closed the door and headed down the stairs. *Those silly feelings I thought I had for Duncan? Well, they were just a momentary weakness—nothing more. I'll keep away from him until I regain my balance. Now there's a bonny plan—full of good sense.* She sighed. *If it is such a great plan, why does it make me miserable?*

Duncan stood at the foot of the stairs. Brigit wanted to spin around and run back up in the pretense of having forgotten something—but that wouldn't be the truth. She squared her shoulders and continued down.

He gave her an appreciative smile. "You're a comely lass, Brigit Murphy."

"Thank you." She tried to brush past him.

"Brigit." He captured her hand and stopped her. "Stop avoiding me."

"I've work to do."

"Yes, you do, don't you?" His deep voice flowed over her. "Emily tells me you made that fine new shirt I like so well. I told her I want a dozen more—all made by you."

She snatched that as an excuse. "With all that stitching to do, I'd best get right on it."

He squeezed her hand, then turned loose. "I'll let you go for now—but we'll talk later."

Brigit shook her head. "We've nothing to discuss."

He dared to reach over and touch a tendril at her temple. "I disagree."

"I'm needed in the kitchen," she stammered. With a total lack of grace and decorum, she dashed for safety.

❧

John glanced up from the newspaper. "Pennsylvania Telegraph didn't mince words today. Listen to this: 'We have no notion or idea that Abraham Lincoln will be defeated as a candidate before the American people for the presidency of the United States; but if such a calamity should occur, it would be the worst blow that ever was inflicted on the laboring men and mechanics of this country. It would arrest our progress in every improvement, by opening all the paths of industry to the competition of foreign and domestic slavery.'"

Duncan nodded and set down the ship's log he wanted to review. "Strongly put."

John folded the paper and slapped it down on the desk. "I've never prayed as hard for our nation as I did when I cast my ballot today."

"I need to go vote." Duncan looked about. "Things are far calmer than I expected. How did you manage to make the men keep their opinions on the vote to themselves?"

"Franklin passed the word: Anyone stirring up dissension or stumping for votes is fired. The men need their jobs too much."

Duncan rested his hands on his hips. "I'm supposin' Gerard O'Leary protested you were curbing his right to free speech."

"Yeah, but Old Kemper nipped that in the bud. Told O'Leary his speech wouldn't be free if he was drawing wages when he said his piece."

"Commonsense men like Kemper would straighten out the political mess in no time." Duncan arched his back to stretch out a few kinks. Em often rubbed John's shoulders to banish the tautness. *Soon Brigit will be my wife, and I'll relish that kind of closeness myself.* He thought for a moment to inform John of his decision to wed, then squelched the notion. He'd given Em his word that she'd be the first to know.

❧

"Miss Emily," Brigit asked that afternoon, "I'm wondering where that lovely little figurine went—the one of the lass in the pretty gown and a lamb at her side. 'Tisn't on the hall table anymore."

Emily looked startled. "That's where it always is. I chose that spot because it's farthest away from the children's rooms and won't get bumped. I hope one of the girls didn't borrow it. It belonged to my sister, Anna, God rest her sweet soul. I'd be heartbroken if something happened to it."

No one confessed to knowing where the pretty porcelain piece went. For a brief instant, Brigit wondered if the man she occasionally saw from her attic window might have taken it; but she dismissed that thought. He'd never even come close to the house. In fact, the times she spied him, he was always by a shrub or next to a tree. Hadn't she overheard Mr. John say he hired men to patrol the grounds? Whoever the guard was, he'd be competent—John Newcomb would engage a bulldog of a man for the sake of his family.

Brigit forgot about the missing statue because she was due for her evening off, and she planned to go visit her parents. Bless Cook's heart—she remembered Mum loved apricots and wrapped a jar of them along with a small crock of whipped cream for Brigit to take home.

Surrounded by her warm cashmere shawl and holding the sweet bundle to give to her parents, Brigit felt blessed. She loved to be able to give even the smallest thing to help them. As she hurried home, she whispered, "Lord Almighty, I'm thankin' You from the bottom of my heart for the ways You provide for my family."

"Hey, there, Brigit Murphy! What are you doin' here?" a lass asked as Brigit turned a corner and headed down the side street toward her parents' building.

Brigit stopped and smiled at the young girl she'd met on the boat as they'd voyaged here. "I'm paying a visitation." She cradled the apricots and cream in her arms and tilted her head toward them. "I've something small that'll be sure to please my mum."

❧

Duncan stood in the shadows around the side of the tenement

building as he heard Brigit speak. When he left the polling place, he'd spotted her bright blue dress and contrasting yellow shawl in the distance and recalled Emily mentioning it was to be Brigit's evening off. Duncan quickly followed Brigit to the edge of town until they reached here and counted his blessings that the Lord presented him with this unexpected opportunity. He needed to know where her father lived so he could obtain permission to court her and seek her hand in marriage. Duncan smiled to himself. He'd rather the courtship part of the arrangement be quite brief and hoped Brigit would feel the same way.

He'd thought 'twas fitting that the woman he intended as his bride would catch his attention. And why wouldn't she? A comely lass she was and quick minded. But in the last few days she'd avoided him. In fact, she'd ghosted away whenever he entered the room. Once she'd been underfoot all the time. No matter where he turned in that house, she'd be there. He smiled. He'd been attracted from the start, and the fact that he'd been so aware of her was ample proof. He suspected the reason why she'd begun hiding from him, and he'd help her get over that shyness. He'd likely scared her with that playful romp at Phillip's party. Soon as he made it clear he had honorable intentions and would safeguard her reputation, the woman would light up his world with her smile once again.

He'd overheard her say something about having a little something to please her mother. Duncan lounged against a tree and folded his arms across his chest. His bride was a dutiful woman. Devoted, too. The mental list he'd started of her fine character qualities kept growing.

He'd have to do something at once about her parents' housing. They'd be his family now, too; and he didn't want them living in this dangerous, squalid place. Duncan didn't even want her in there right now. He thought to ask which room her parents rented, but a trollop approached him and offered her services.

Duncan shook his head. "I'd like information is all."

"It'll cost ye." The tart gave him a coy smile.

"Brigit Murphy—do you know what room or floor her family is on?" He placed a coin in the woman's hand.

"I couldn't say. There are Murphys aplenty, so I don't bother to keep them straight. Brigit doesn't live here. She's hired out in service to a fancy family." The trollop gave him an assessing look. "You'll have to tell me. Has old Mr. Murphy done something wrong? Is there a reward for him?"

"No. Not at all."

She heaved a sigh. "I didn't think so. They're one of the goody-good families. Her da walks her back to the grand place where she's a maid; my da turned me out to make money."

Duncan looked past the rouge and gaudy clothes. "If you were offered a decent job, would you give up this way of life?"

She shook her head. "Sinnin' suits me fine. Money's not bad, either."

Her attitude left him feeling soiled. Duncan straightened up and walked off. He'd found out what he needed to know. Brigit's father would return her safely this evening, and Duncan planned to wait for him.

He went home with a sense that his life was about to change—and for the good. Aye, 'twas a grand feeling. He'd have a wondrous wife, a fine ship, and if the election went as he'd voted, the country would have a wise man at the helm.

The minute Duncan entered the house, Goodhew took his coat and told him in a grave tone, "Mr. John and Miss Emily wish to speak with you at once. They're in the upstairs parlor."

Well and good. I'll tell them of my plan to wed Brigit. "Thank you, Goodhew."

The minute he entered the small upstairs room, Duncan knew something was wrong. Em's eyes were puffy and red. John stood by the window, tension singing from every last inch of his frame. Duncan shut the door. "What is it?"

"We have a thief in the house."

thirteen

"A thief?!" Duncan echoed the words in disbelief.

The fire in John's eyes made it clear he'd determined the truth.

"Who is it?" Duncan demanded.

"I haven't pinned that down yet." John grated, "But as soon as I do—"

"I'm really not sure anything's been stolen," Emily confessed. "I could have misplaced my cameo, and I recall allowing Anna Kathleen to borrow my fan. She mightn't have returned it."

Duncan let out a relieved gust of air. "Is that all?"

"No." John cleared his throat. "I've left money out on purpose—and, I confess, not a single cent of it has been taken."

"I'd think money would be the first thing to be taken. If it's left alone, then perhaps Em's right and those other things are simply misplaced."

John sat next to his wife and took her hand in his. Duncan could see how hard he was trying to contain his anger so Emily wouldn't suffer any more upset than necessary. He waited. John wasn't a man to jump to conclusions. He was probably doling out the bad news a bit at a time to soften the impact on Emily.

"A book I'd been reading seems to have grown legs and walked off, and you know about my grandfather's fountain pen. Anna Kathleen told Emily today that her locket is missing, too. None of those things alone amounted to much of anything. In fact, most of them could have simply been misplaced. Emily and I decided to keep watch, but we said nothing since we've never had cause to mistrust the household staff."

Emily whispered, "We were hoping things would turn up again." She gave Duncan a look that melted his heart. "But now our Anna's pretty little statue is gone."

He jolted. "The shepherdess?"

Emily tearfully confirmed, "Anna cherished it so."

John thumped his fist on his thigh. "Julie's china doll is gone. The truth is clear enough: The stolen goods are ones a woman would want. Whoever's taking them has to have free access to the house. That means—"

"The thief is on staff," Duncan finished. He shook his head in disbelief. "Let's try to put together the pieces of the puzzle."

"Goodhew and Cook have been with me forever." John stared at the door. "My grandmother hired them, and they've served faithfully for decades."

Duncan agreed. "No suspicion could be cast in that direction."

"That leaves the maids," John said grimly. "Em and I were trying to apply some deductive reasoning before you came in. Trudy and Fiona can scarcely read, so it makes no sense that they'd take a book or a fountain pen."

"But since you might have just misplaced those, we can't rely on that." Emily tugged on his hand. "You've been so busy that you're a wee bit absentminded, you know."

"Fiona is patient as can be with the girls, so she'd have ample opportunity to take a doll; but she's awkward as a pelican," Duncan thought aloud. "I can't imagine her tiptoeing around—she'd crash into something first."

"Trudy's made a pest of herself mooning over Duncan," Emily told John. "I've been keeping my eye on her or assigning her to tasks along with another maid so she'd be supervised. I'm doubting she could have managed to pilfer anything."

"That leaves Lee and Brigit." John's face tightened. "They can both read."

"We have to trust them." Emily looked from John to Duncan and back again as she asserted, "I do, I'm telling you."

Duncan shoved his hands in his pockets. It had to be Lee then. His sweet little Brigit wouldn't ever—

John forged ahead. "I've been trying to put the facts together. Lee was gone on her days off when the locket and cameo were taken. That leaves Brigit."

Sick anger washed over Duncan. *I trusted the lass. I was ready to make her my wife. How could I have been such an idiot? She's been playing me for a fool all this time.* She'd been clever and quick about helping him over a rough spot or two with Emily's matchmaking—but now he realized she might well be a woman well accustomed to keeping secrets. 'Twas also a way she turned him into an ally so he'd drop his guard and not be suspicious. Oh—and that habit she had of slipping her hand into her apron pocket that he'd thought was so endearing—was it a sinister thing? Had she been swiping things from under his very nose?

Recalling the bundle she'd carried into the tenement to-night only fanned the flames of Duncan's mistrust. Hearing her boast that she had something sure to please her mother—well, that about cinched it.

Brigit—she'd duped him as easily as John's brother, Edward, had gulled Anna. *At least I discovered the truth before the marriage. Thank the Lord for that small miracle. This is already debacle enough as is.*

Duncan felt as if he'd swallowed a fistful of barnacles as he agreed, "It's Brigit."

"No, it can't be," Emily insisted. "I trust her. You must, too."

"Trust? You expect me to trust her? Em, I saw her carry a bundle into a building tonight. Before she disappeared, she boasted about how she had something to please her mother. It's plain as can be what's happening."

John stood. "I'll dismiss her this minute."

Emily tugged him back down. "You're jumping to conclusions—that's what's happening. Why, Brigit is the one who pointed out the figurine and the doll are both missing."

"It sure seems like more than a simple coincidence that Brigit 'discovers' the items are gone. It's nothing more than a smokescreen. It's her way of looking innocent while she's probably pocketing the goods and pawning them."

"It doesn't make a lick of sense. We've countless things a thief could take that would bring a far better price than what's come up missing."

"Let's talk about what's missing." Duncan struggled to get Emily to face the facts. He felt as if he'd been gut-punched and understood her shock; but pain was best dealt with right away so they could get rid of the problem. . .get rid of Brigit. "Think about it: Nothing ever got taken until she came to work here."

"Brigit has a pure heart. She'd not take a thing, I'm telling you." Emily folded her arms across her bosom and glared at him. "I know my staff."

"She has you bamboozled."

"Do I come down to your vessels and pass judgment on the men you hire for your crews?"

"Em," John said in an I'm-trying-to-be-patient tone, "that's an entirely different matter."

"Indeed it is." She agreed all too quickly. "Here at home if I employ a bad staff member, the worst that can happen is that some little trinket is taken; if you sign on a man who does something wrong out at sea, it can cost lives."

Duncan refused to try to reason further with her. Until his sister came to her senses, he'd have to protect the family from Brigit's pilfering. "I'm going to shadow her and see what she's up to. What we need to do is keep this quiet. The best way to catch a thief is to let her think she's safe. If she doesn't suspect we're wise to the problem because she's taking only paltry items, she'll keep at it. I'll catch her red-handed."

"Josiah is hale again." John nodded. "You can stay home, and he'll take the *Contentment* out since you just did his run with the *Cormorant*."

"It won't be necessary. I'll do this next run with my crew. Mark my words—it won't take long to get proof on"—he saw the look on Emily's face and hastily changed the end of his sentence—"the thief."

Emily heard his plan and let out a humorless laugh. "You've far better things to do with your time. I'll make no bones about it: You've lost your mind. If you're searching for anything at all, your wits ought to be at the top of the list."

Duncan stood and left the room. As he shut the door, he thought, *If only it was just my wits. I've lost my heart.*

fourteen

Da walked her back to the Newcomb estate and gave her a kiss on the cheek. Brigit hugged him tightly and whispered in his ear, "I love you, Da. Take care of Mum."

"I worry about you." He looked up at the mansion and shook his head.

Brigit's heart beat heavily with the sadness she felt. Not so long ago, Da had been the owner of such a fine home. Aye, he had. Now he couldn't even land a steady job. She gave his hand a squeeze and tried to lighten her tone. "Worry? Now there's a fine waste of your time. You're supposed to lay me at the Lord's feet and not fret a bit."

She went upstairs to her attic room and waved out the window until Da was out of sight. A quick splash at her basin, a quick change into her warm flannel nightgown, and she had a bit of time to read her Bible. After she closed it, she blew out her lamp, walked to the window, and stared out at the ocean as she prayed.

The Lord's world was vast. Aye, and He could reach out His mighty hand and do anything. *Tonight, heavenly Father, I'm asking You for just a small thing. Insignificant really. Well, it is important to me. Please, will You help Da to come into his own here in America?*

After she finished praying, Brigit continued to look outside. A sudden movement caught her eye. There he was again—the man who sometimes crept to the very edge of the trees and shrubs before the clearing around the house. He stood there in the dark of night. Once she'd seen him there at the break of dawn.

Who is he? Is he the man Mr. John said would be patrolling the property? Can it be in connection with the private meetings Mr. John and Duncan held about the possible war? She'd seen the crate filled with fine wooden boxes down in the corner of the library. Titus had gotten snoopy and opened one while she was dusting. Because of that incident Brigit knew the boxes each contained a fancy-looking firearm. It all probably linked together.

Brigit balanced on one foot and rubbed the back of that calf with the toes of her other foot. War. Politics. She wrinkled her nose. Such matters were for men. She needed to mind her own business.

In the few seconds she'd not paid attention, the stranger disappeared. Someone was walking straight toward the house. She pressed her face closer to the window pane and squinted. Oh. It was Mr. John. Clearly, whomever he'd met wasn't of any danger to the household. Since Mr. John saw fit to slip out of the house and hold his meetings in the dark, Brigit decided 'twas best she ignore them. Aye, that was what she'd do. She'd forget she ever saw a thing. Maids were supposed to ignore, disregard, and overlook any matter that wasn't set squarely in front of them. She'd do just that—especially because she liked the Newcombs and wanted to be the best maid they'd ever employed.

&

"Oh, let me guess: Emily's gearing up for her holiday entertaining." Duncan sauntered into the dining room and smiled at Goodhew and Brigit.

"She does this every year. It wasn't much of a guess," Goodhew said to Brigit.

"I heard that!" Duncan drew closer to where Brigit sat on the floor in front of a massive oak and marble buffet. He gave her a playful smile. "Maybe you can explain it to me. Why do women think they have to put the food and drinks in these fancy dishes? Men just want a plateful. In fact, if the plate is full, we can't very well tell if it's a fancy one or a plain one."

"Ladies don't fill their plates." The twinkle in her eyes let him know he'd managed the right approach.

"But who cares about the plate as long as the food on it tastes decent?"

"The ladies do," Goodhew said with a sigh. "Which is why I'm doing inventory. It's just as well. I'll need to replace a few things."

"Is something missing?" Duncan forced himself to sound only passingly interested.

"Just a cup here or a plate there—the ones the children managed to chip or break. That lovely, rose-shaped silver tray is gone, but it's because Mrs. Waverly declared it was hers after a church tea and carried it away. Miss Emily was too much of a lady to squabble over it."

Duncan took the lid off a crystal candy dish and popped a gumdrop into his mouth. He offered the dish to Brigit and Goodhew; both declined, so he set it back down and helped himself to another before replacing the lid. "Do we have enough trays then?"

"Eight," Brigit reported. "Eight silver trays. Miss Emily has as many china ones—lovely, hand-painted ones. The two glass ones bring the total up to an even dozen and a half. We haven't even looked at the large trays yet. I'm thinking she has trays aplenty."

Duncan slowly chewed the gumdrop. "Enough that she won't miss one or two?"

Brigit smiled at Goodhew. "She'd probably not miss them, but Goodhew certainly would!"

Goodhew nodded urbanely at that praise. "Thank you, Brigit. Now how about the chafing dishes?"

Brigit dipped her head and walked her fingers on the rims

of some silver pieces. "There are four chafing dishes and four—no, five—pairs of candlesticks."

Duncan watched as Goodhew scribbled the figures on a pad of paper and nodded.

Brigit leaned into the piece of furniture and took a closer look. "I'm thinking the candlesticks are wanting a good polishing. They're showing tarnish about the bases."

"You're right. That simply won't do. We'll see to that later, after the inventory. The Newcombs always host a New Year's Eve ball. All the families from the shipping company are invited. We'll need the punch bowl. Do you see it?" Brigit scooted a bit closer to the other edge of the cabinet. "Which one? There are two in here. One's all silver; the other's silver and crystal."

"Emily prefers to serve the punch in crystal and wassail in the silver." Duncan went back for more gumdrops.

"I'm thinking that would look quite festive." Brigit reached into the center of the nested punch bowls. "There's something in here." She carefully unwound a length of red velvet.

Cook came in the room. "Ah, look! You found the dinner bell." She bustled over and grabbed it. She rang it a few times and smiled at the clear, high tinkling tone. "Isn't that the prettiest little thing you ever saw? Years ago, when 'twas just old Master Newcomb and John living here, I'd use that to summon them for meals. I don't remember why we stopped."

Goodhew took the bell from her and handed it back to Brigit. He gestured for her to wrap up the bell and put it away. "The children make a fair bit of noise. Especially with the lasses playing the piano, the bell simply wasn't practical."

"They both play well." Brigit put away the bell and shut the cabinet. "Miss Emily said the twins will begin lessons soon."

"I need to speak to Miss Emily," Cook said. "We've just finished counting the linens."

Duncan watched Brigit tense. He'd done the same thing.

The butler looked at his wife. "Is there a problem?"

"Not exactly. It's all there. It's just that a few of the table linens are showing wear, and the one from supper is hopelessly stained. It'll have to become a picnic blanket. Miss Emily will want to replace them."

"I'm a fair hand at stitching." Brigit stood, closed the buffet doors, and discreetly dusted off the back of her skirts. "If those pieces need only a bit of mending, I could see to them."

"I can attest to that from the shirt Emily had you make for me."

Brigit flickered a quick smile of thanks.

"No use wasting your time on old tablecloths, Lass." Duncan glanced down at the shirt covering his chest, then back up at her. "Your efforts would be much better spent by sewing more of those fine shirts for me, and I brought home material for just that purpose."

Cook snorted. "You're a scoundrel, Duncan O'Brien. This very morning I told Miss Emily the staff is needing new aprons. Don't you be thinking to steal away Brigit and her needle."

Sticking to the truth always worked best, especially when spinning a web. Duncan let out an exasperated sigh and looked at Brigit. He waggled his brows playfully. "She's right. I am a scoundrel, and you'd best be warned."

He left the room, pleased as could be. Brigit had just gotten an eyeful of things that any thief would happily snatch, and she seemed quite relaxed. It shouldn't take long at all now.

❧

Brigit dusted the downstairs and hummed under her breath. She looked at the gumdrops and scrunched her nose. Duncan was an odd fellow. He'd picked out the black ones. Aye, that was the only color he'd eaten. She should have accepted one—she could have put it in her pocket and given it to Mum. Too late now. She wasn't about to invite herself into the Newcombs' candy dish.

The library was the last place she'd need to dust. She saved it for last because the scent of the place always brought her such an intense longing for home. The mingling of smoke from the fireplace, the leather from the countless volumes on the shelves, lemon and beeswax furniture polish—'twas her idea of what heaven might smell like.

Top to bottom, one side to the other. Dusting didn't take any concentration—'twas a grand chore for that very reason. Brigit enjoyed having a chance to be alone with her thoughts. In fact, she liked having a chance to be alone.

Especially after having been around Duncan awhile earlier, she needed to remind herself of a few choice facts. Duncan had been pleasant and polite to her in the dining room, but he was that way with everyone on the staff. When Trudy ended up falling from the stairs into his arms, hadn't he made sure she wasn't hurt before he set her down? When Fiona asked him to read a letter from home to her, hadn't he stopped what he was doing and read it twice, so Fiona could relish all the news? Aye, Duncan O'Brien might have a devilish smile, but he had the heart of a choirboy.

Brigit rolled the ladder toward the left side of the far wall and climbed up. As she dusted, she tried to rub out any personal thoughts of Duncan. She needed her job, and the fastest way to lose it would be to be moon-eyed over him.

The door opened as she climbed down at the right end of the row. Duncan and Timothy entered. Timothy held a book and exclaimed, "I thought the punishment was cruel."

"Why is that?"

"Because she bore it alone, and she couldn't have gotten with child unless—"

"Why, Brigit," Duncan interrupted his nephew. "So you're dusting in here, too?"

"I have the downstairs today. Would you gentlemen prefer for me to come back later so you can have some privacy?"

Duncan gave her a keen look. "You've done a fair bit of reading. Have you read Nathaniel Hawthorne's *The Scarlet Letter*?"

She could feel the heat rush to her cheeks. "It was given to me as a gift. I ceased reading it when I came to realize the nature of the subject."

"Sidestepping the indelicacy, do you agree with Tim that the punishment was cruel?"

"From what I recall, it seemed unnecessary." Brigit chose her words carefully. "The child's existence made the issue clear."

"Exactly," agreed Timothy.

"What of other crimes and punishment?" Duncan leaned against the desk. "Say. . .theft. What would be reasonable?"

"I've read that in some places in the world," Tim said with relish, "they cut off the thief's hand."

Brigit shuddered in horror. She turned back to continue dusting. The whole time she worked in the library, Duncan and Timothy carried on a lively conversation about various forms of punishing criminals. Duncan managed to use examples of discipline problems aboard a sailing vessel. He capitalized on the opportunity to mentor Timothy and give him advice on how to maintain control. His theory of discipline versus punishment held merit. Brigit found herself thinking Captain Duncan O'Brien undoubtedly earned his men's allegiance fairly.

❧

Duncan felt restless. Surely something would happen soon. He'd made certain Brigit viewed things she could easily steal and pawn. For awhile he'd almost forgotten himself. He'd managed to track Brigit into the parlor and immediately snagged the twins as an excuse to go in and monitor the maid. Brigit ended up teaching the girls a simple tune on the piano. When they'd each learned it, she set them a few octaves apart and let them play it as a duet. They made up several silly lyrics to go along with the music, and Duncan had to admit Brigit was quick to find a rhyme and had a sense of whimsy.

She'd also not forgotten to do her tasks; because once she had Julie and June set up on the piano bench, Brigit flipped the cushions, plumped the pillows, and rolled up a rug. Not long thereafter, Duncan saw her fling that very rug over a line and beat it. Cold as it was outside, she'd come back in with rosy cheeks.

He refused to be beguiled by her pretty face. Sooner or later she'd slip up, and he'd know it. Duncan sensed that time was at hand. He'd retired to his bedchamber, but rest eluded him. Duncan finally took off his shirt and shoes yet restlessly prowled until he got rid of some of his energy. At long last, he looked out in the hall, yawned, and left his door ajar. He didn't bother to fold back his bedding—he lay atop the counterpane and dozed.

The slightest rustle and click woke him.

fifteen

Brigit woke to a shout. She yanked on a robe and hastened into the hallway. Lee, Trudy, and Fiona stumbled from their rooms, too.

"Did someone die?" Lee quavered.

Trudy ran for the stairs. As she struggled to yank open the oftentimes stubborn door, she wailed, "If somethin's a-wrong, I'm finding Duncan. He's strong enough to protect me!"

Fiona tromped down the stairs, fluttering her hand under her nose and muttering, "That perfume she's wearin' is strong enough to revive Goliath and make him keel over dead a second time."

By the time Lee and Brigit reached the second floor, the family was up and standing in a knot by the master suite. The children were in nightshirts, and Miss Emily's flannel nightgown peeped out from beneath her roomy shawl. Mr. John had his arms around Miss Emily, who was weeping.

Duncan wore a pair of black britches and a blacker scowl. He folded his arms akimbo and spoke through gritted teeth. "We've been patient far too long. Enough. Enough, I say. Whoever's the thief, confess now."

"Thief?" Trudy's gasp conveniently bumped her right up against Duncan.

Duncan righted her and took an aggressive step forward. He shoved the children behind his back. "The ring. I want it now."

"What ring, Unca Duncan?" Phillip asked as he scratched the cowlick at the back of his head.

"Anna's wedding ring." His voice rivaled a thunderclap.

"Anna's got a wedding ring?" Fiona yawned. "That makes no sense at all. The lass isn't even betrothed yet."

"Timothy's mother was named Anna," John said somberly. He continued to shelter his wife in his arms and rub his hands up and down her back. "Emily kept the little gold band in a special place. It was to go to Timothy's wife someday."

"No further explanations," Duncan rasped. "Everyone is to go to his or her room. One at a time, you're to visit the necessary. Open the laundry chute, then close it. Whoever took the ring is to slide it down the chute. We'll not be able to determine who took the ring, so you can keep your wicked little secret."

Emily wiped her eyes and quavered, "Whoever took it, I just want it back. If you're in dire straits and needed money, you could have come to me. I'd have willingly helped you. I still will. Please—just give back Anna's ring!"

Brigit blinked to keep from crying along. She swallowed hard and held her hands tightly together at her waist. She'd once had a ring—a pretty little emerald Mum gave her for her thirteenth birthday. What a treasure it had been—a symbol of her becoming a young lady. When they'd arrived in America, Da barely had any money left. Brigit sneaked away the second afternoon and pawned her ring. They'd eaten three meals before Mum noticed Brigit's ringless finger. The memory still tore at Brigit—not because of the sacrificed ring, but because of the anguish on Mum's face. Miss Emily looked as bereft as Mum had.

"Back to your rooms now." Duncan looked fearsome as could be, and Mr. John had his hands full, trying to calm Miss Emily.

June stared up at her uncle with saucer-sized eyes and tugged on the leg of his trousers. "I'm not big enough to open the laundry door."

Julie added, "Me, neither."

Duncan's craggy face softened for a moment as he bent down and rumbled, "Now there's a fact, but I'll not fret over it. Neither of you is tall enough to have reached the ring in the first place."

Titus poked Phillip in the side. "That leaves you out, too, Shrimp. You're too short."

"Am not!"

"Are too!"

"Boys!"

Phillip got up on his toes and stood shoulders-to-ribs with Titus. "I opened it before and threw Julie's do—." He cut off the word and flushed brightly.

"Phillip, you'll keep those feet on deck here." Duncan set his hand on the lad's shoulder to make his point. "I'll deal with you about the doll."

Emily pulled away from John. "Phillip, did you take the ring?"

"Why would I want some stupid, old, girl's ring?"

"The rest of you go to your rooms," Duncan ordered. "In ten minutes you're to start making your trips to the laundry chute."

❧

"No ring." Duncan paced in the library. He wheeled around and frowned. "How did you and Em both sleep through someone sneaking into your room?"

"We weren't in the room." John cleared his throat. "Em— well, I'd carried her to the necessary. She's not feeling her best in the early mornings. It looks as if you're going to be an uncle again."

The news stopped Duncan in his tracks. He looked from his brother-in-law to his sister and back. "Well, I'll be switched." For a moment he grinned. *Babies. Em loves babies. But at her age? I'm almost twenty-one. That makes Em. . .thirty-five.* A surge of anger swelled. "That does it. You can't have this kind of upset in your delicate condition!"

"Delicate?" Emily let out a watery laugh. "Family, yes;

delicate, no. I'm healthy as a draft horse. I'm just so s—sad that s—someone is embarassed to c—come—" She dissolved into tears again.

"Whoever it is isn't embarrassed; she's wicked. And we already know who it is, so let's stop beating around the bush."

John jerked to attention. "You saw who took it?"

"No, but I told you and Em—"

"He made a wild accusation when he said 'tis Brigit." She sobbed into John's chest as she clung to his shirt. "I know he's wrong. I just know it."

Duncan heaved a sigh. The last thing his sister needed was for him to add to her agitation. He gave John a look, and John nodded. They'd take care of it later. Duncan then said as softly as he could, "Our Emily, don't be in a dither. I won't do anything rash. You have my word on it."

She lifted a tear-stained face to Duncan. "Stop sounding as if I made you gargle vinegar, Duncan O'Brien. This whole thing is a tragedy, and I'll not have you add to it by accusing an innocent. No, I won't."

He had no trouble giving her his promise. "I won't harm an innocent." *I'll catch Brigit red-handed.*

❧

The uneasiness in the house was palpable—between the election results and the theft, everyone was on edge. Miss Emily had Goodhew call the staff together while John was at work and the children were at school. Brigit watched her as she pasted on a tremulous smile.

"I've lived through lean times, and I know what a strain it can be. Each of you is a valuable part of this household. I've decided since it's too hard on someone's pride to ask for help, the best thing to do is intervene. Instead of having distrust and tension, I'm simply increasing everyone's salary."

Goodhew sniffed. "I'll not take a cent more. I won't be painted with that extortionist's brush."

Everyone else started to chime in, but Miss Emily held up a hand to silence them. "No one is to speak of it again. Not a word. I've made a decision, and it's a condition of your employment."

Brigit shook her head. She'd never seen such a sad set of circumstances—or so she thought until later that afternoon when she was clearing away the luncheon dishes. Poor Miss Emily had no more than risen from the table when she collapsed into a dead faint.

Trudy let out a screech.

"Stop that noise and go fetch Goodhew," Brigit commanded as she raced to Miss Emily's side. She immediately loosened the throat of Miss Emily's gown and chafed her hands.

A shadow fell over them, and Duncan boomed, "What did you do?"

Brigit glanced up at him. "She swooned. I don't know why."

He scooped Miss Emily off the floor and headed for the stairs. "Fetch Cook to help me and have Goodhew send for the doctor."

Trudy, Cook, and Goodhew arrived at the same moment. Cook must have spilled something in her haste. The front of her dress and apron were drenched. "I'll see to her," Brigit volunteered and hurried up the stairs right behind Duncan.

As soon as he settled his sister on the bed, Duncan turned his back. He rasped, "Loosen her. . .dress improver. She oughtn't be wearing one in her condition."

Brigit gave fleeting thought to ordering him out of the chamber. It wasn't proper for him to be there. It wasn't even proper for him to allude to such an intimate issue. Squabbling with him wouldn't tend to Miss Emily, though. Brigit quickly unfastened Miss Emily's gown, unlaced her corset, and covered her with a blanket. She then dipped a cloth in the pitcher and draped it over Miss Emily's forehead.

Duncan wheeled back around. "Leave."

For the next three days the young captain who once sparkled with humor and intelligence prowled around the house like a hungry panther, ready to pounce. Brigit counted the days until he set sail again. The man was wound like nine days on a seven-day clock.

Brigit's heart went out to Miss Emily. The poor woman was distraught, and she didn't do well at hiding that fact. Oh, to be sure, she tried; but 'twas clear as an icicle that her feelings knotted her something fierce. Brigit tried to do tiny things to ease Miss Emily's sadness. She made an effort to open drapes to let in the weak wintry sunshine. She hummed lilting tunes. Cups of tea, an unasked-for footstool—anything Brigit could think of, she did for Miss Emily.

Phillip, the wee scoundrel, had taken Julie's doll and dumped her down the laundry chute. He'd confessed that rotten deed; yet the pretty little china doll never ended up in the laundry bin in the basement. Duncan brought in a small grappling hook. He cleverly dropped a rope down the chute, tied the hook to the end, and slowly pulled it upward. By doing so, he recovered Fortuna Hunter.

Later that day Brigit saw Duncan tinkering with sliding more things up and down the chute. She figured he'd come to the same hope she had: Mayhap the ring had been sent down the chute and got lodged as the doll had. Her hopes soared, then crashed as Duncan finally slammed the chute and stalked away.

❧

The world was turned upside down. Folks seemed to want to pick on one another. To hear half the folk talk, President Lincoln was the devil incarnate; the other half would drag a chair up to Christ's right side for him. Slave and free, rich and poor, North and South—strife and contention fulminated just beyond the property line. Until now it had stayed there—but the peace of the Newcomb home and life were no longer assured.

Duncan watched for an opportunity to restore that peace. He'd not managed to nab absolute proof that Brigit was the thief, but every last fact pointed toward her. He'd heard the rustle and click before he discovered Anna's ring had gone missing. The door to the servants' quarters in the attic clicked. He'd checked, and it sounded like the noise he'd heard. Then, too, the very last maid down to see what the ruckus was about just so happened to have been Brigit. She must have taken a few moments to hide the ring.

Duncan gave consideration to tearing the attic apart to locate the ring, but it was such a wee band, it could be in countless places—many he'd not even consider. As soon as he proved her guilt, he'd force Brigit to reveal where the ruby ring went.

Aye, 'twas she. Logic gave firm reason to rule out every other member of the household staff.

Emily pointed out that Phillip swiped Julie's doll, and they'd all presumed it had been stolen. Most of the other items were minor and could easily have been misplaced. But she couldn't explain away the figurine or the ring.

John vacillated between trusting Emily's judgment and wanting to fire all the maids. Because it would upset Em too much, he didn't want to tilt her precarious peace of mind based purely on conjecture.

Waiting. Of all things, Duncan counted patience among his weakest traits. A man of action, he hated to stand by and let time pass without doing something. Clearly something needed doing.

sixteen

Brigit cleaned the windows in the library. I should have traded with Trudy. I could be scrubbing the tub instead of this. Then I wouldn't have to be here, remembering how Duncan O'Brien hid in here, trying to escape from Miss Emily's marriage candidates.

Deeply troubled by the shadow hanging over the household, Brigit tried to banish any worries or suspicious thoughts. She'd done nothing to earn anyone's distrust or animosity. Duncan alternated between being his suave, clever self and rumbling with all of the fearsomeness of thunder. 'Twas a crying shame he'd lost his peace.

Oh, he'd not outright say so. A man had his pride and didn't want others to know when things bothered him. It was just that Duncan never seemed much of a mystery to her. From the day she'd been a coconspirator by keeping his presence in the library a secret, she'd thought they'd gotten along well enough. Reading his thoughts came as easily as scanning a newspaper. The only problem was, Brigit kept getting the wild notion he was watching her.

Miss Emily kept telling her to go the extra mile, to be sympathetic about the pressure Duncan was under. What with the political matters at a near boiling point and the frustrations of dealing with supplies that weren't arriving on time for the ship building, Duncan simply wasn't himself—at least, that's what Miss Emily said.

On top of all of that, they were having foul weather. Men pontificated about how the Farmer's Almanac rightly predicted this relentless stream of storms, and Brigit had felt the icy sting of the sleet on several occasions. For the past few days, the temperature dropped even farther, and they'd experienced snow. Surely, for the men to be working out of doors gave adequate cause for Duncan to come home in a black mood.

Since he'd announced a thief was in the house and spilled his ugly thoughts, Brigit had become increasingly self-conscious. Thoughts about finding a new position filled her mind; but with the uncertainties in the political climate and the facts that she had no funds upon which to fall back and her parents relied on her, she had to stay. Brigit decided to keep vigilant. She loved Miss Emily and wanted to help put an end to this travesty. She'd do it because it was the right thing to do, but also because Miss Emily had been so kind to Mum and Da.

Mum and Da looked so pleased when she'd brought what Cook called "the autumn baking crate." Why, with just a bit of meat and eggs, they'd have most of what they needed to eat for quite some time. Aye, and that extra jar of apricots Cook gave—Brigit nearly cried with delight over how good the Lord was to add that extra bit of sweetness to her parents' life.

She'd been giving almost all of her pay to them when she visited on her day off. Da picked up a day job here and there, but mostly bosses wanted to hire stronger, younger men. The voyage over left Mum frail of health. She'd not last a month if she took on any labor. Each day Brigit woke with a sense of gratitude that God provided this job.

Beautiful things filled the Newcomb estate. Aye, the home boasted grand rooms with fine appointments. Upkeep on such a place was a never-ending proposition. Miss Emily kept the staff busy. In the past two days she'd taken to giving orders here and there that should have been customary; but what with the suspicion that a thief might be in their midst, the chores took on a different flavor. The tensions stretched tight.

Brigit swiped at a tiny streak along the edge of a pane. For all she'd endured until now, she'd always found contentment in her circumstances. She suspected Duncan O'Brien felt that same way. Whoever was behind the robbery had stolen Duncan's serenity as certainly as he'd taken all the goods.

Worn out from yet another busy day, the entire household retired early. Brigit stood at her attic bedroom window and fidgeted. When Duncan came home, he'd been in a good mood—as if the sea winds blew away the worries he'd carried when first he set sail. Now he hovered. Every time she turned around, he seemed to be there. His smile didn't reach his eyes, either. Like a lightning bolt, the realization struck her as she mopped the floor tonight. *He's hunting for the robber, and he thinks I'm guilty!*

Holy Savior, what am I to do? I can declare my innocence, but what would that accomplish? She rested her forehead against the icy pane and blinked back tears of frustration. A pair of verses from the twenty-fifth chapter of Proverbs ran through her mind. *"If thine enemy be hungry, give him bread to eat; and if he be thirsty, give him water to drink: For thou shalt heap coals of fire upon his head, and the LORD shall reward thee."*

Feed Duncan. Fill his glass. Be kind. *Such seemingly simple things to do—but with the suspicious way he's behaving toward me, Father, those acts will take every last shred of my will and a boatload of Christ's love to accomplish. I don't want to obey Your holy Word only to keep my job. If I did that, 'twould be living by law and not by grace. I'm praying now for wisdom and a forgiving heart. Help me, Lord. Help me minute by minute. I cannot do this on my own.*

Sleepless, she continued to stand at the window. A slight movement caught her attention. She spied the stranger she'd seen on those other occasions in the yard. She couldn't tell much by the weak moonlight, but maybe he was involved somehow. *I simply cannot stay silent about seeing him any longer. If he is a guard, he's had to have seen something; if I've been wrong about presuming he's a guard, then I need to get one of the men to capture him.*

Brigit's heart pattered as fast as a toe-dancer's feet as she slipped into a wrapper and ran to the servants' staircase. She grabbed the knob and twisted, but the door refused to open. The stubborn thing wouldn't budge.

"Oh, no!" She tried twice more, each second pounding with her heartbeat. *He'll get away. I'm fiddling with this stupid door, and that man is getting away!*

Frustrated and unwilling to let the matter alone, she dashed back to her room. Ignoring the icy weather, she opened her bedroom window and crawled out onto the roof. Slick it was, and so cold, it felt burning hot beneath her hands and knees. Normally Brigit rather enjoyed looking out her window, but looking down from this vantage point didn't give her any pleasure—it nearly scared the wits straight out of her.

She tried to recall the house's floor plan. Could she go right and drop down onto one of the children's balconies? No, wait. Right would be Duncan's—well, she did need to get him. She stood and wobbled. Clumps of snow slid away and made soft, distant *plops* as they hit the ground. She started to pray aloud, "Dear Lord Almighty, don't let me turn into one of those plopping sounds myself!"

Cold. Oh, cold, cold, cold. Each step she took made her shiver worse. Brigit strove to keep her footing as she crossed the roof, then groaned as she drew close to a chimney. In her effort to keep from slipping right over the edge, she'd gone too far. Both arms stuck out to help her balance, she looked behind her. No. She couldn't possibly turn and go back. She'd barely kept alive going straight ahead. Turning all the way around would be pure folly. "Lord, You know I'm not here to kill myself. Aye, You do. I'd take it kindly if You'd grant me deliverance."

The trellis—the very tips of a trellis stuck up beyond the edge of the roof. She whispered her thanks to the Lord, then swallowed hard. He'd given her a way down, but it wasn't going to be easy. Then again, how many times had Da said most of the good things in life didn't come easy?

Sure she'd skid right over the edge if she took another step, Brigit took a deep breath to steel herself. As it was, she slipped as she laid down on her belly with her feet toward the dropoff. Her fingers scrabbled for any hold, but it was a vain effort. She skidded over the edge and barely muffled her shriek as she caught the trellis and held on for dear life.

For a second she closed her eyes. "God, don't stop now. I need Your help, and I'm needing it badly." She opened her eyes and saw violets. Violets? Oh! Her gown and robe were hooked on the trellis—as if God had snagged her there for safety's sake! She had to hold on with one hand while she freed her slushy garments with the other. The clammy fabric slapped at her legs, and she shuddered. When she got hold of Duncan and he apprehended the stranger because of her tremendous effort, that man was going to owe her at least a dozen apologies.

It being winter, the vines on the trellis were dried-out, rough things. Nary a leaf remained—something Brigit counted as a blessing, because she'd end up slipping on them or wearing them if they'd been present. The whole trellis wobbled, and she didn't waste time. It might snap.

She also hurried because she needed Duncan to nab that stranger. The longer it took her to alert Duncan, the greater the chance was that the intruder would slip away.

"Fine thing for a young lady to do in the dead of winter, in the middle of the night," she muttered as she climbed down. "'Tis nothing short of a miracle I haven't broken my neck."

A big, rough hand clamped around her ankle. "That could still be arranged."

seventeen

One quick yank, and Duncan pulled Brigit off the trellis. He caught her—a chivalrous thing to do, all things considered. The mud puddle there would have been a just reward for her perfidy.

"Duncan!"

"Surprised?" He clamped a hand over her mouth and hauled her toward the kitchen. He didn't want her crying alarm and warning her partner. Hopefully, John would catch him. It took every last shred of decency for Duncan not to shake her senseless. What had she taken this time, and to whom was she going to pass it?

Just tonight, after everyone else went to bed, he and John had a quick exchange. The two of them concocted a solid plan to capture the thief once and for all. Duncan no more than set foot into his bedchamber and went to shut a crack in the curtains when he saw a bit of snow slide over the edge. It wouldn't have been anything to catch his attention, but then several more followed. Realizing someone was on the roof—of all things!—he ran outside.

He could scarcely believe his eyes. *Brigit.* Regardless of what logic told him and the way he'd been behaving over the last two weeks, deep in his heart, Duncan secretly still fostered a thread of hope that she was innocent. The thread snapped, and the full weight of her betrayal hit him. He'd trusted her with his family and almost with his heart—he'd been ready to propose! Anger mixed with incredulity. He nearly bellowed her name, but cold reason washed over him. If he startled her, she'd likely slip and break her neck; he wanted the satisfaction of doing that deed with his own hands—not that he would, but the thought satisfied a savage need inside of him. Besides, if he made a noise, he'd scare off her accomplice.

For having been as skilled as she'd been with her other episodes of theft, she wasn't smooth this time at all. The daft woman had let out a shriek loud enough to wake Methuselah, then muttered to herself the whole time she scrambled down the trellis. No doubt about it, the woman had a death wish.

Now Brigit didn't act innocent. No, she surely didn't. She squirmed and struggled—even tried to bite his hand. He got her in through the kitchen door, kicked it shut, and bumped into the counter ere he reached the table. The whole while, Brigit gave him more grief than a tiger in a burlap sack.

He dumped her onto the table where Cook usually kneaded bread. Keeping his hand firmly over her mouth, he anchored Brigit in place by clenching the belt to her robe. "Don't you make a sound."

She reached up and closed both hands around his wrist. Though she tried, she couldn't yank his hand away. Before Duncan could imagine the depth of her desperate insanity, she turned loose and threw herself backward. A tug and loud rip ensued. Within a second, she ended up in a heap on the floor; he stood with a soggy belt to a flowery robe in his hand. He tossed it aside and dove after her. She smacked at him and yelped, "You're letting him get away!"

Duncan pinned her to the floor. "Let me guess: He won't even bother to come after you. Regardless of the cliché, I've found there is no honor among thieves. You're going to have to shoulder the blame yourself."

❧

Brigit stared at Duncan in disbelief. Here she was, trying to unravel the mystery and catch whomever it was that had been robbing this good family of their treasures. What happened? Duncan considered this as proof that she was the guilty party.

She glowered at him. "While you're wasting time with that ridiculous notion, the thief is making his escape!"

"I'll settle for one of the pair." He reached across her and grabbed the torn belt. Quick as could be, he grabbed both of her wrists in one of his massive hands.

"If you—" She tugged against him, but to no avail. He had her well and truly bound, knotted faster than a schooner in a gale.

"Be silent, or I'll use the other length to gag you."

Duncan stood and lifted Brigit to her feet. He pulled out a chair and nudged her into it.

Nothing he did made sense. He'd actually been quite gentle when he'd lifted her; and the minute he had her seated, he hastily jerked the flaps of her robe shut. How could a man have the mind of a jackal and the manners of a saint?

She started to shiver. Her soggy garments, bare feet, and the unheated kitchen combined to make her miserable. Brigit swished her head from side to side, trying to get a swath of hair that worked free from her braid to cease drooping over her left eye. All she succeeded in doing was to whip herself with the wet plait.

"Fighting won't get you anything." Duncan scowled. "Now tell me who your partner is, and where can I find him?"

Utterly frustrated, she glowered back. "I don't have a partner because I'm not a thief. I was coming to get you because I saw a man in the yard!"

"So you nearly broke your neck, crossing the roof in order to reach me."

"The door is jammed. I had no choice."

Duncan shook his head, skepticism painting every last feature.

"That's right. Go on ahead and scoff. You've been pointing your finger at me, and I was working to prove my innocence. I had to do something—as long as that villain is free, you'll keep blaming me."

"Obviously for good cause," he said in a voice rich with vindication. "An innocent person wouldn't be sneaking around at night, and I caught you dead to rights. I won't let anyone steal from my family."

"Neither will I. You're falsely accusing me; and if I do nothing, it'll cost me my job. You'll be stealing the very bread out of my parents' mouths!"

eighteen

"Hush!" He barked the order in a hoarse tone. Memories of his young years—of his family being cold, hungry, and sick flooded Duncan's mind. He'd not yet reached his seventh birthday, but he'd known things were dire. Even so, Emily never once stooped to thievery. Duncan held no sympathy for this maid.

"But—"

"I'll not listen to another of your lies. You've betrayed the trust and kindness of this family. Don't try to justify it by trying to earn my pity or sympathy with sad tales about your family's woes. The truth stands—"

"Aye, it does!" Brigit stared him straight in the face.

Tears glossed her eyes, but fire burned in her cheeks. She'd been caught, and 'twas nothing more than embarrassment and anger that caused this reaction. Duncan refused to be moved by her words.

He yanked out a chair, slammed it down next to her, but failed to take it. "Not another word out of you. John will be here soon, and I'll have him waken Emily."

Brigit's gasp only fired his temper more.

"Oh, yes. Emily will be told. You couldn't believe we'd leave her ignorant of your role in this. The children will have to be warned, too—so don't think you can weasel your way back into anyone's good graces—not after what you've done."

"I'm telling you, I didn't do anything!"

Duncan scoffed. "If you were innocent, you'd still be sleeping in your bed—not climbing down a trellis at this hour.

John will have to determine whether to turn you out or turn you over to the authorities."

As if on cue, John came into the kitchen. He lit a lamp and stared at Brigit. "There are tracks out in the mud. Most have a dusting inside them, so I know they're left over from the party. There is one set that's fresh. I saw a man, but he ran before I could get close."

Duncan noticed Brigit's fiery denial of guilt didn't settle any better with John than it did with him. She pled that she'd never steal—not as an upright Christian woman and because she needed to keep her job so she could provide for her parents.

John's jaw hardened as he stared at her. "You're giving yourself plenty of motive."

Brigit lifted her chin in a dignified manner that was at direct odds with the lock of hair hanging down her face and her spongy garments. "Supposing you men are right. Try explaining why I'd be risking my neck to walk across a snowy roof when I don't have a single treasure on me!"

Duncan gritted his teeth. She had a point. He'd not caught her red-handed.

A rustling in the doorway made Duncan and John whirl around. Emily entered the kitchen with a shocked look on her face. Brigit couldn't help herself. "I didn't do anything wrong, Miss Emily. Honest, I didn't!"

John hastened to his wife's side. Tears streaked down her cheeks, and she clutched him. "Come on, Sweetheart. I'll take care of this."

Emily shook her head. "Something's wrong."

"I know, Dear. Duncan and I are handling this. You go on back to bed."

"But everything's back." Emily gave her husband a bewildered look. "Up in the hallway. There's a towel, and everything that's been stolen is on it—the statue and the cameo and our little Anna Kathleen's locket and your book—it's all there except my sister Anna's ring."

Duncan couldn't bear to see Em cry. She rarely wept—except during the months when she was carrying a babe. Then she cried enough to float an armada. He would process the information about the returned articles in a few moments. For now he intended to block Emily's access to Brigit. Tenderhearted as Emily was, she would—

"What is that odd sound?" Emily's tears were tapering down to the hiccup stage, and she pulled away from John.

Duncan and John took a quick looked at one another, then both focused on the same thing at the same time.

"Look at the poor girl!" Emily ran to Brigit's side and quickly flipped back the silly lock of hair to expose the maid's pale face.

At first, Duncan thought her lips were quivering in a theatrical attempt to earn pity; but then the truth dawned. Her teeth were chattering. Even then the noise wasn't from that. It was because her chair rattled on the floor from her shivers.

"You've scared the lass." Emily looked down and let out a breathless shriek. She fumbled with the binding. "You've tied her! Undo this at once."

Duncan yanked a knife from the butcher block and sliced clean through with a single swipe. He kept a hand on Brigit's shoulder. Originally it was to keep her from trying to bolt, but now it was to keep her from falling out of the chair. He frowned at her. The woman felt cold as sleet.

As he was in just shirtsleeves, Duncan didn't have a coat to offer. He swept Brigit into his arms and growled, "Em, you come along and see to it she changes." He headed up the stairs with his sister pattering directly behind him. When they got to the stairway to the attic, Em managed to open the door without the least bit of effort. Duncan shot a yet-another-lie look at Brigit. It was wasted effort. The lass huddled into a ball in his arms. Aye, she did—but at least she exercised enough intelligence not to cling to him.

Emily went ahead of them and opened the third attic bedroom door. A blast of cold met them. Brigit had left the small window open, and the room felt like the inside of an icehouse. While Duncan lowered Brigit onto a bed she obviously hadn't slept in, he rasped, "Emily, don't shut the window. The floor may be slippery over there, and I don't want you to fall and hurt yourself."

"Nonsense." The window slammed shut. "We need to warm her up at once."

He straightened, turned, and wagged his forefinger at Emily. "No arguments. Make sure she dresses warmly and pack the remainder of her belongings. You have five minutes."

Temper had him wanting to bellow the words, but discretion demanded he not. The last thing he needed to do was wake the whole household. Emily needed a chance to accept the betrayal before everyone else was told. He went back to the stairs.

The door stuck.

❧

Brigit wrapped her shawl more closely about her shoulders. *Lord, I'm in such a mess. What am I to do?*

Duncan carried her valise and kept one hand clamped around her elbow as he led her down the road. Brigit refused to say a word. She didn't dare. The minute she opened her mouth, she'd humiliate herself by weeping. Her boot hit a rut, and she started to tumble, but Duncan jerked her upright.

"Are you all right?"

She couldn't bear to look him in the eye. Right about now she'd vow the boots he wore hid cloven hooves. How could she once have believed him to be charming and kind? If anyone was guilty of deceit, Duncan O'Brien topped the list.

He stopped. "I asked if you were all right."

She nodded. He let go of her elbow and tilted her face up to his. He stared at her but said nothing. Brigit turned away from his touch and started to walk again.

"No." He took hold of her arm and drew her the wrong direction. "Come this way."

So that's the way of it. Mr. John wanted me thrown out of the house at once. He couldn't even wait until sunrise to get rid of me. They were just pacifying Miss Emily with the tale of Duncan giving me a ride into town. He's really going to take me to the edge of the estate and send me on my way. Brigit swallowed, but the big lump in her throat didn't move. The sooner she put some distance between herself and this place, the better. She walked alongside Duncan in absolute silence.

"You're still shivering. That shawl isn't warm enough." He started to remove his thick, brown greatcoat.

Brigit bit back a cry. The last thing she wanted was to be wrapped in this hateful man's garment. "Leave me alone." She sped up until she was nearly running.

Duncan caught her in a few strides. "Slow down before you slip again." He gained a better hold of her, and his voice took on a rough edge. "You'll stay with my parents at the care-taker's cottage. They've just returned home from a long trip. I'll arrange for the rest of the staff to think you're here to help my folks air out the place and spruce it up."

Brigit shuddered. Her reputation was in tatters, and she'd never get another job without references. What would happen to Mum and Da?

Duncan opened the unlocked door to the caretaker's cottage and nudged her inside. She could barely see the embers glowing on the hearth. He led her over to a settee and whispered, "Lie down here. I'll stir up the fire."

Woodenly, she seated herself in the corner of the settee. She watched Duncan's broad back as he squatted at the hearth, added kindling and a pair of logs, and brought the fire back to life. Even when the room radiated with its warmth, Brigit couldn't stop shaking.

Duncan walked behind the settee. He spoke in low tones to someone, but Brigit was too stiff to turn and couldn't understand what was said. A few moments later, Duncan stood before her and unfolded a thick quilt. He draped it around her shoulders and managed somehow to raise and twist her so she was bundled in it. By the time he finished, he'd laid her down and robbed her of her shoes.

❧

Duncan decided to spend the night in the wingback chair. He could keep watch over the fire and Brigit. He'd been so sure of her guilt. John seemed convinced, too. But Em—Em vouched for Brigit's goodness.

And that attic door stuck.

Then that moment out on the road changed everything. The ache in Brigit's eyes nearly knocked him to his knees. In that split second, everything settled in his mind. He knew for certain this woman—the woman he still loved—was innocent.

From the time he'd started dealing with business, Duncan discovered he'd been given a gift of discernment. He could sense the character of a man and determine whether or not to hire him or contract his services. Even weasels like the sail maker knew better than to try anything shady with him. From the first time he saw Brigit, he'd seen the goodness in her. Aye, he had. She'd filled his glass with milk that time, then gone on to fill his heart with sunshine.

But he'd been a fool. In his rush to avoid marriage, he'd not trusted the gift the Lord gave him. It took a voyage away from Brigit to make him come to his senses; but once he returned, he let the octopus of doubt nearly strangle him. Looking into Brigit's eyes, he'd seen the truth. Oh, he had.

She was innocent; he was guilty. His heart had been right from the very start, and he'd been a fool to allow circumstances to cloud his judgment and test his love. He'd hurt her because of it.

He had a lot to make up for.

Duncan hadn't followed John's edict to get rid of Brigit at once. He'd made up his mind, and John could bluster all he wanted. Until Duncan could prove Brigit was blameless, he was going to shelter her reputation and feelings by having her live with his own parents. He'd vouched for her innocence just now when he told his parents who she was and why he'd brought her here.

It had taken a long while for her to fall asleep. Silent tears streamed down her face until she did. Though Duncan knelt by the settee and tried to reassure her, she'd been too far gone to hear a word he said. Between cold and shock, she just lay there and trembled. Mama had offered to brew tea, but Duncan doubted Brigit would be able to swallow it. Papa cleared his throat, beetled his brows as he looked at Brigit and hesitantly suggested, "Medicinal brandy or whiskey might do the trick."

So on top of all of my mistakes, I'd give Brigit the humiliation of thinking I'd made a sot of her.

He shook his head. "Rest. What she needs is her rest."

"I'll go make up the bed in the spare room."

John had added a fair-sized bedroom and a workshop onto the other side of the kitchen years ago, but Duncan shook his head again. "Mama needs her rest, and the fire here's what the lass needs more than anything."

Both of those statements were true, but they were only an excuse. He couldn't bear to leave Brigit alone in this calamity. Even after she fell asleep, he couldn't stand to be more than just a few feet away.

Still alarmed at how cold she'd become, Duncan tiptoed

over to make sure she'd warmed up. Even though Brigit lay exactly where he'd put her, she'd managed to curl into the quilt tighter than the coil in a seahorse's tail.

At least the shivering stopped. He counted that as a good sign. He'd have to settle for that one sign, because nothing else looked very promising. Dried tears pasted wild strands of her ebony hair to her face. Just days ago, playing with the children in snow had caused those same strands to form springy tendrils around her hairline. He tenderly fingered the strands. *Lord, help me make this up to her. Help me make things right.*

Duncan went back and took his station in the wingback chair. Thoughts swirled in his mind. He had no right to claim his love for her until he earned her trust. He'd nearly shattered her with his accusations, and a sensitive woman like Brigit would need time to get over such ugliness. The best thing he could do was show his support for her and prove her innocence. Once he did, God willing, she'd become his bride.

Sweat rolled off his forehead, but Duncan popped another log onto the fire. Purgatory probably felt cooler than this parlor, but he refused to risk Brigit's catching a chill. Finally he settled back into the chair and decided he could afford to doze. On the slim chance she woke up, Brigit wouldn't be able to get away. He had her shoes beneath his chair. Even more he had her in his heart.

nineteen

"You did what?" The force of John's bellow could have filled every last sail on a clipper.

Duncan didn't mind the bluster. He'd expected it. Locking eyes with John, he said very clearly, "I took Brigit to my parents' cottage. She's staying with them until this matter is cleared up."

"It's already solved, and I won't have her on my property."

"She's not on our property, Dear," Emily whispered. "You gave the cottage to my parents. It was very generous of you. You did it right after you added on that nice, big second room."

"This isn't a game." John glowered at them.

"No, 'tisn't," Duncan agreed. "I'm saying here and now, Brigit is the woman I love. The devil can have a holiday in a suspicious mind, and I was fool enough to let him—but no more. We have no proof against her. None. What I do have is my faith in her and in the Almighty."

Emily yanked on John's hand. "John—"

"Don't be taken in by love, Duncan." John gave him a world-weary look. "Remember Anna."

"If I would have minded that advice, I'd have never wed you," Emily said quietly.

Duncan nodded. "I'll prove Brigit's innocence; and once I do, I want her welcomed back with open arms. She's going to be my wife."

❧

"Christmas is just around the corner." Nonny O'Brien's cheerful announcement didn't much lift Brigit's spirits. Not wanting to cast a pall over Duncan and Emily's mama's happy mood, Brigit plastered on a smile and nodded.

"We want to celebrate the holiday in the Old World way. I ken 'tis an imposition, but I was thinkin' to ask for your help." Soon Nonny had Brigit firmly entrenched in her plans. They sewed doll clothes for the twins, painted a whole fleet of ships for Phillip, and polished up little jewelry boxes Papa O'Brien made for the older girls.

Being involved in those holiday customs helped Brigit regain a few shreds of her serenity. She always loved the holidays, and she could see how much Nonny and Papa loved their family by the affection in their eyes and voices and how they lavished thought and time into making a special gift for each grandchild. Brigit knew the children would be delighted.

Truth be told, Brigit had a second reason for looking forward to Christmas. Duncan's new vessel would be finished any day. As soon as Christmas was over, he was due to take the ship on her maiden voyage. From what she'd overheard, she gathered it would be an extended voyage. She needed to have time away from him.

Duncan came by each day and promised to prove her innocence. To his credit—or was it Emily's?—the rest of the Newcomb staff had been told Nonny O'Brien needed Brigit's help with several Christmas projects. It was the truth, but Brigit felt it was only a half-truth, and such things made her squirm. What else could she do, though? At least she'd not been subjected to public scrutiny or shame, and every bit of her salary still came so she could take care of her parents.

Mum would take one look at her and know something was dreadfully wrong, so Brigit didn't want to go home. Bless his heart, Papa O'Brien delivered the money to her parents and came back with a handful of cheerful stories and the assurance that all was well with them.

Someone pounded on the door. Brigit ran to answer it.

The minute she saw who stood there, she wanted to slam it shut. Duncan's arms were full of fabric.

"Emily's asked if you'll make new gowns for the staff."

Brigit stared at the two huge bolts of material and blinked to be sure it wasn't her overactive imagination. Indeed it wasn't. Miss Emily hadn't sent solid cornflower blue serge or wool. No, she hadn't. She'd had her brother deliver a dainty green-and-white ivy print and a stunningly feminine, very stylish pink cabbage rose.

Duncan stood in the doorway and gave her an amused look. "You needn't decide betwixt the pieces, if that's why you're hesitating. Emily wants you to make a gown from both fabrics for each of you."

"My. Oh, dear me. Yes, well. . ." She backed away from the door and gestured for him to come in. *I've been a bogbrain, leaving him out in the cold.*

Duncan conscientiously wiped off his boots before he stepped over the threshold. He carried the bolts over to a small table on the far side of the parlor and propped them up against it. After making sure they wouldn't slide and fall, he set down a small wooden case. "There you are."

When he turned back around, Brigit forced herself to keep her hands folded at her waist. "Miss Emily chose bonny cloth, to be sure."

"So you like it?"

Brigit nodded. She didn't want to prolong the conversation. In fact, she wished Nonny would come out of the kitchen and ease this dreadfully awkward encounter.

Duncan took a seat and made himself at home. Brigit wanted to shove him straight back out the door; but it wasn't her home, and she had no right. He'd dropped by at least once a day since she'd come here. Now 'twas a good thing for a son to be dutiful and loving. Clearly he displayed both of those laudable qualities toward his parents—but he'd been checking up on her. He and she both knew part of his intent was to hover like a hungry hawk, and she was the field mouse he'd nab if the merest opportunity presented itself. Oh, he'd said he intended to prove she was innocent, but Brigit's trust in him was too badly shaken to allow her to believe him.

"Em sent you the whatnots in that case." He leaned forward and rested his elbows on his knees. The man looked comfortable enough to stay a good long while. "She wanted to be sure you had everything you needed."

At your request, so I wouldn't steal? Brigit held her tongue. Regardless of how upset she felt, antagonizing him wasn't right. "Please let Miss Emily know I'll get to sewing at once."

"My sister is a bit distracted these days. If you find you require anything else, just let me know."

Brigit nodded.

Duncan must have figured out she didn't care to pursue a conversation because, after silence stretched between them, he stood. He walked toward the door and stopped directly in front of Brigit. "You didn't catch a chill from the other night?"

He sounded almost concerned. Brigit could scarcely credit it would matter to him at all. Likely Miss Emily wanted to know. Staring at his shoulder, she said, "I'll save the scraps for the girls' sewing baskets."

Duncan made an impatient sound and tilted her face to his. Before he could speak his mind, Nonny's laughter sounded from the other side of the room. "Nonsense. You'll keep those scraps yourself. Duncan-mine, I'm wanting a wee bit of satin. The palest blue, if you have it—just scrap is all. About a yard or so will do nicely." She came over and patted his chest. "Drop it off whenever's convenient."

"I'll see to it." After giving his mother a quick and sure hug and kiss, he left.

Brigit went to the fabric and touched it.

"I'll have ye know, our Duncan chose those prints," Nonny

said in a gay lilt. "Our Em had him get them in Lowell. You'll be a pretty sight in that green, come Christmas."

"I'll be sure to make up that print for the girls first."

Nonny shook her head. "Dinna be thinkin' you sneaked that by me with your sweet vow. You're to make one for yourself, too."

Brigit busied herself with some housekeeping, then ventured toward the small wooden box. Inside were needles, thread, scissors, a tape measure, a slip of paper with everyone's measurements, and a thimble. Another bit of paper had been folded and wedged into the lid.

> *"Blessed are ye, when men shall revile you, and persecute you, and shall say all manner of evil against you falsely, for my sake. Rejoice, and be exceeding glad: for great is your reward in heaven: for so persecuted they the prophets which were before you."*
> MATTHEW 5:11

Brigit folded the verse and tucked it in her pocket. *God, please bless Miss Emily and Nonny for their kindness. To be sure, I'm in the fiery furnace; but You gave them to me just like You allowed Shadrach to have Meshach and Abednego with him during his trials.*

Over the next week, she took out the slip of paper and read the verse over and over again. Oh, she knew that verse. Back when she was but a small lass, she'd committed it to memory. That was all well and good, but now it served two purposes: It prompted her to keep her eyes on the Lord in her troubles, and it reminded her someone still had faith in her honesty.

Duncan continued to drop by. Sometimes he had a good excuse—like with the blue satin. He'd brought by no less than five different shades of blue so his mother could make a

choice that suited her fancy. There was no mistaking it—
Duncan O'Brien cherished his family.

Most times he just came by. He didn't seem to have any
reason at all, but Brigit knew the truth—he was there to
intimidate her and spy on her. She tried to make herself
scarce during his visitations, but that wasn't very easy in the
small cottage. She felt clumsy as a cow with him around.
Awkward and fumble-fingered as a twelve-year-old lass, and
all because he made her so self-conscious. Every last thing
she did fell under Duncan O'Brien's scrutiny. Each time he
left, she'd breathe a sigh of relief.

Working helped keep her mind off her troubles. Brigit stayed
industrious from the minute she woke until Nonny O'Brien
chided her into blowing out the lamp at night. She already had
Cook's and Lee's dresses nearly finished, and she'd cut out
Fiona's and Trudy's today. As both of them were identical in
size, it made more sense to tackle them at the same time.

After having cut out all of those gowns, Brigit still had
cloth left. . .cloth originally earmarked for her. She wouldn't
make it up. No, she wouldn't.

That night she waited until Nonny and Papa went to bed;
then Brigit sat by the hearth and carefully embroidered.
When her eyes grew too weary, she tucked away her stitching and turned in for the night. After she blew out her lamp,
she climbed into bed and curled into a ball of misery.

Da always said God had a purpose for everything. Aye, and
he also said anything worthwhile was hard won. *Lord, I don't
understand what I'm supposed to be learning from all of this.*

A faint, scraping sound interrupted her prayer.

Brigit slid out of bed and threw on her robe. Her bare feet
made no noise on the floor as she crossed into the doorway.
A man had nearly folded himself in half to fit through the
window; but when he turned, a shaft of moonlight illuminated his face.

He was the man she'd seen out in the yard all those nights!

Brigit didn't even pause to consider her actions. She ran across the room and used the seat of the chair as a stepping stool in order to leap onto the man's back. She wrapped her arms around his neck and legs about his waist as she screamed, "Help!"

Papa O'Brien ran out and managed to belt the intruder in the middle.

The door crashed open, and Duncan thundered in with a bellow. Brigit continued to cling to the stranger as he wheeled around. Papa was in midswing and couldn't stop. He accidentally knocked her off. She hit the wall as she saw Duncan lunge and heard him hiss, "You!"

twenty

The tide had come in late that night, and Duncan needed to be there to meet a vessel. He'd ordered special gifts for John and Emily, and he didn't want them to find out. As he rode by his parents' cottage, he heard Brigit's screams. He vaulted off his mount and tore through the front door.

Seeing her hit the floor made his heart stand still. Seeing Edward made his blood run cold.

The uppercut he served Edward hit true, as did the blow to his middle. Edward crumpled over; but the odd part of it was, he'd never put up the slightest defense. "Fetch some rope," Duncan barked.

"I know where there's some," his father said, panting. "Just a minute."

"Brigit? Are you all right?" Duncan knelt by her and bit back a roar as she dazedly lifted her hand to her head. "Come here, Sweet." He scooped her up and carried her to the settee. He didn't want to turn her loose or put her in the other room. He refused to let her out of his sight, but Edward's moan let Duncan know he couldn't turn his back for a single second.

"I've got her, Son." His mother patted his arm.

"Rope." His father came back into the room, holding aloft a fair length. "Good sturdy rope 'tis. We'll bind him to a chair."

Duncan thrust Edward into the chair and set to work. He yanked the rope tight and knotted it once more for good measure. That task done, he wheeled around and strode to the settee. His mother was clucking over Brigit, whose wide eyes and pale face made his heart lurch. A quick glance at the spot on Brigit's temple told him she'd have a headache and a good-sized lump for a day or so. Even so, he couldn't resist cupping her cheek. "Are you all right?"

"I'm fine."

"No, you're not," he rasped angrily. "Stop sitting here. Lie down. Da, I'm asking you to go fetch the doctor."

"I don't need a doctor."

"Nonsense." Duncan lifted her and cradled her for an instant to assure himself she'd not really been hurt any other way. "There's a knot on your head, so you're not thinking clearly. I want you lying down until the doctor says you can get up."

"Then lay her down," his mother urged.

"I'm deciding where to put her. She's cold. Look at how she's shivering."

His father crossed the room. "You left the door open and let in the winter night air. I'm thinking that's as good a reason as any for the lass to be shivering." He slammed the door shut.

Brigit jumped and winced at the noise.

"I'll go into town and get the doctor," his father said, "but I'm yanking on my boots first."

Duncan studied Brigit's features. "Are you seeing double or feelin' like you might lose your supper?"

"The only double I'm seeing is that man," she whispered. "He looks like John Newcomb."

Duncan murmured some nonsense to calm her, then settled her back on the settee. He shed his greatcoat and covered her in the depths of its thick brown folds.

"You turned into a fine young man, Duncan," Edward said softly. "You treat a lady well."

"At an early age, I saw you do the opposite." Duncan shot Edward a venomous look. "I learned my lesson from that."

Unable to tolerate the sight of the man who had betrayed

his loved ones, Duncan strove to contain his temper. He strode to the window and stared sightlessly out into the yard. Since the day he'd learned Edward duped his sister Anna into a sham marriage and abandoned them, Duncan had longed for justice. In a flash of characteristic honesty, he admitted to himself he wanted more than justice—he wanted revenge.

"You killed Anna. Aye, you did." He didn't turn to make the accusation. "Granted, you never actually plunged a knife into Anna or shot her—but you did worse when you deceived and betrayed her. You left her, knowing she carried your child. Aye, you left her to freeze and starve.

"Here, in this very cottage, Anna passed on. She passed on shamed to the depths of her soul, her heart broken because she finally learned of your betrayal."

The cottage stayed chillingly silent. Finally Edward confessed, "Everything you say is true. I cannot begin to—"

Duncan's father slammed his fist into something. "Then say nothing."

Duncan clenched his jaw at the wave of sorrow that washed over him. His arms shook with the effort it took to keep his fists at his sides.

"What more did you plan to take from my family?" he demanded in a low roar of fury. "Haven't you already done more than enough?"

"I have." Edward's voice carried no challenge. "And I—"

Duncan wheeled around. "Why? Why did you come back here? And spare me your lies. I've had a belly full of them already."

"I've told more than my share of lies. I came here tonight to try to make right a small portion of my wrongs."

"Impossible."

"There's an envelope in my pocket. Read the letter. You've nothing to lose by reading it."

Duncan's father jerked the envelope from Edward's pocket. He strode to the fireplace and almost threw it in, but Edward shouted, "No! Anna's ring is in there!"

"Anna's ring! What were you doing with that? You had no right." Duncan grabbed the envelope and opened it with a savage rip. He cradled the thin golden band with the tiny ruby chip in his palm. He hadn't seen it since he was a lad, and the broken promises it represented washed over him. "You put this on her hand with deceit in your heart. You're not worthy to touch it."

"You're right. I'm not worthy." Edward bowed his head. "I'm a sinner of the worst sort. I have no excuse for the evil I did, and any apology wouldn't erase the wounds I inflicted."

Duncan's mother stopped dabbing at the bump on Brigit's temple. "Then why did you come back?"

"Because God sought this lost sheep. I'm in the fold of Christ now—bought by His precious blood. Only now can I look back and admit the wrongs I've done." He shook his head and sighed. "Anna loved me with all her heart."

"Aye, and you broke that sweet heart of hers," Duncan bellowed.

"I did. I'm ashamed of that. Though the Lord has forgiven me, I don't ask it of you. I have no right. I've come to realize what a treasure I had and gave up in Anna."

Father moaned. Mama sniffled.

Duncan glowered. "Some new leaf you turned over. You found another lass, teamed up, and stole. So tell me now who you had in the house as your accomplice."

"I have no accomplice." Edward shook his head. "I sneaked into the house. There are passageways built in the walls where I've hidden. I discovered them when I was a boy. I took the things I'd given Anna—not so I could keep them, but because I've had replicas made of them. I wanted to have reminders of her."

"You don't deserve—"

"I don't. But it wasn't a matter of justice. I wanted to ensure Timothy would get the ring; and while I was looking for it, I happened across some of Anna's other things. I found I longed for a touchstone—memories of the few times in my life when I'd been happy. She did make me happy, Duncan. I gave back everything I took."

"You're a liar. You took more than just Anna's things, and you kept back this ring." He held out his hand to display the unmistakable evidence.

Edward cleared his throat. "I took the other things so you wouldn't notice a pattern. I gave it all back, except the ring. The letter is written to Timothy. I wanted him to have the ring, hoping someday he'd be able to give it to his sweetheart. The joy on Anna's face when I put that ring on her finger—I want my son to see that same joy on a girl's face someday."

"Tim's an honorable man. When he weds, it will be a true marriage, and he'll provide and protect as a husband should."

"That knowledge pleases me. I pray my son turns out better than I did."

Duncan sucked in a deep breath. Edward wasn't saying a word in his own defense. He clamped his teeth against the vile things that wanted to spill out, then unfolded the letter.

My son Timothy,

It's a sad day when a father's first words to his son are an apology and come only after the boy has already grown into his manhood. You deserved better.

I'm only now writing this, not contacting you in person because I gave up any right to you when I abandoned your mother. I was a sinner of the worst sort. Anna was an innocent, and her very goodness drew me to her. She gave me her heart, and she pledged her love. It shames me to say I took all she so freely gave, then left her.

God took Anna home, and I knew about you. Though I acted hard-hearted, I felt such deep shame that I wanted you spared my influence. Emily and John had fallen in love, and I knew they'd rear you far better than I could. All these years you thought I'd spurned you; the truth is, leaving you was the one sacrificial act of my life. Seeing the young man you've become gives me peace about that decision.

My conscience has haunted me all these years. The Holy Spirit wouldn't allow me ease. God, our Good Shepherd, sought me. He untangled me from the brambles of bad living and redeemed me by the blood of the Lamb.

Two years have passed, and my walk with the Lord has deepened. I came to a point where I knew that though I'd been forgiven, I still had to make restitution for my wrongs.

When I left, John told me I'd be welcomed back if I got right with God. I came back fully intending to be a prodigal brother. That night, though, I heard you in the garden, pouring your heart out to Duncan. I realized then that I couldn't return home because the cost of my reunion would be far too great, and you would be the one to bear it.

I deserve nothing. Still, over the years, I've come to realize the days I shared with your mother were the sweetest of my life. Looking back, I now know I loved her—as much as a selfish, evil man could. The one thing I wanted for you is the legacy of love Anna carried in her heart. The day I put this ring on her finger, she glowed. By all rights it should be yours to give to your sweetheart someday. Let it always remind you of the constancy of unconditional love.

I wronged you and am worthy of your resentment and hatred. There are no words to say how sorry I am. Forgiveness is a sacred thing, something only God or His children can grant. I was unworthy of His mercy; yet He granted absolution. My sins were cast into the depths of the sea. Timothy,

you will sail those seas. It is my hope that you will not let my
sorrows and sins burden you and cause your spirits to sink.

Anna is with the Lord; and by the Savior's mercy, I'll see
her in heaven someday. It is my prayer you will serve God
and live a rich, full life, so I can finally see you face to face
in paradise.

Edward Timothy Newcomb

Duncan finished reading the letter aloud.

"I want nothing from you," Edward said softly. "I just wanted to leave the letter and ring here. I've made a life for myself—one that is full, save the fact that it is lonely. Wealth, I've discovered, is empty when love is absent. I've set up an account for Timothy, and he's named as my sole heir."

"Your money willna mean a thing to the lad," Duncan's mother whispered tearfully.

"I don't expect it will. It's all I have to leave him, though."

Brigit was trying to muffle her sobs. Duncan strode over to her. The poor lass looked woozy and overwhelmed. He shouldn't have allowed her to stay in the room and witness this private business, but it was too late now.

"Ah, Brigit." He pulled a kerchief from his pocket and dabbed at her cheeks. "Your poor head. It must be aching something fierce."

"'Tisn't that at all. It's none of my business, but it's all so verra tragic."

"You've such a tender heart. I'm sorry—"

"I'm sorry, too." She clutched his hand. "I've read the newspapers and heard people talking about a coming war where brother would fight against brother. The war already came to this family. 'Tis more than enough to break my heart."

Duncan let out a deep sigh. "There's already been enough hurt, hasn't there?"

Brigit nodded. The action made her draw in a sharp breath

and close her eyes. Her grip tightened as more tears seeped from beneath her lashes. The sight of it made Duncan want to roar, but she whispered, "He's not defending his reprehensible actions. He called himself a sinner and confessed."

"Stop fretting over that now. You're hurting."

Her eyes opened, and a touch of a smile tugged at her lips. "It would take far more than a mere bump to bother a hard-headed lass like me, Duncan O'Brien. Go pay attention to the important things."

"I am."

Her brows puckered. "What are you planning to do about him?"

Arguing with her wouldn't accomplish anything, and he did need to make some hefty decisions. "This has knocked the wind out of my sails. I need some time alone to pray." He turned loose of her hand and tunneled his arms beneath her. "Let me carry you into the other room. My mother will stay with you. Da will go fetch the doctor."

Once he was alone in the room again with Edward, Duncan didn't feel ready to talk. He knelt by the fire and whispered, "Father, he's done such awful things."

They're all forgiven.

"He killed my Anna. Tim's been without a father."

Anna is with Me. I'm Tim's eternal Father, and I gave him John so he'd have a godly man as his example. You are there for Tim, too. Will you teach him bitterness and vengeance, or mercy and grace?

"How can I forgive Edward? I've carried hate in my heart for him all these years. I didn't think I had, but I have. Seeing him here brought back everything."

Forgive him as I forgive you, My son.

Time passed; and for every thought and protest Duncan had, God met him at the point of his hurt.

Slowly Duncan stood to his feet. He went to Edward.

"Knots aren't just things in ropes. They're in hearts and souls and memories." He took a knife from the table. "I don't want to be bound by them any longer." He sawed through the rope. "God's grace and mercy go with you, Edward."

twenty-one

Absence doesn't just make the heart grow fonder—it makes me a bit crazy. Duncan stood in the entryway and scanned the stairs and open doorways, hoping for the impossible: to catch Brigit. The doctor ordered that she stay in bed for a few days due to the bump on her head; and once those days were up, she had come back to the big house. John had insisted on making a personal apology and escorting her back himself. Duncan felt more than a little surly about that second fact. He'd looked forward to having at least a few minutes to walk with Brigit and speak to her privately.

It's been nigh unto a week, and I've seen only that woman's back as she scurries off. I saw more of her when I had her living with Da and Mama.

Oh—evidence of her presence surrounded him. The scent of her perfume lingered in rooms. Swags of pine and holly she'd made festooned the house both inside and out. Ribbons and wreaths had always been a tradition, but this year they abounded. The twins spent hours on end at the piano, plinking out the simple melodies to two Christmas carols Brigit taught them. Duncan wanted to enjoy the holidays before he set sail. It was difficult to, though. Each time he tried to get near Brigit, she slipped away. It used to be that he couldn't avoid her. Then he'd needed to make a bit of effort to stop by his folks' each day to check on her and enjoy her company. Now that she was back in the main house, he could barely find her.

Emily didn't help one speck, either. Just about the time Duncan would locate Brigit and approach her, Emily would call her away or send someone to summon her with a ridiculous matter that was "urgent."

"Emily." He closed the parlor door, shutting his sister in. "We need to talk."

"Very well." She handed him a tiny key and pointed toward the window seat. "Open that. I have something I need to hide in there."

He removed the pink-and-cream-striped cushion and unlocked the hinged lid. "What is this all about?"

Emily laughed. "Since the first year I married John, I've used this as my hiding place for Christmas gifts. It's the one place nobody ever bothers. John bought Timothy a sextant, and I need to tuck this in before someone finds it. We thought that was a fitting gift for him this year. Don't you agree?"

Duncan didn't bother to open the handsomely carved wooden box to admire the piece. He'd let Tim have the honors, then speak his praises on Christmas. "You always make fine choices." After he took care of that matter, Duncan sat Emily down and held her hands in his. "Em, I want you to stop interfering."

"Inter—"

"Don't you dare try to play innocent. I know you far too well."

She huffed. "You're impossible to please. You told me you weren't ready to settle into marriage and insisted I cease what you called the 'petticoat parade.' Well, I have, and now you're not satisfied."

"You look entirely too pleased with yourself," he muttered.
"I am consistent. I've told you not to interfere, that I'd choose my own wife."

"Wife?" Emily gave him an innocent look.

Duncan squeezed her hands and let go. "You'd try the patience of a saint, Em. I've made up my mind, and I'm going to win Brigit's heart. I can't very well do it if you keep hindering me. Stop helping her get away from me."

Patting her slippered foot on the floor, Emily gave him an impish smile. "It took you long enough. How many unsuitable lasses did I have to march past you before you finally figured out the perfect woman was under our verra roof?"

"You were trying to match me with Brigit all along?"

"Isn't it just the funniest thing in the world?" Emily smoothed her skirts. "You're so very much like my John—you live in a gentleman's world, but you work with a rowdy crew. Brigit comes from a fine family. They eventually lost everything due to the famine, and she's been supporting her parents by working here."

Duncan moaned.

"Aye, Duncan-boy-o. She's well educated and cultured, but she never once minded putting her hand to any task—however small or dirty it might be. She'd been here only two days ere I wondered if she'd be the one for you. The night you and she shared that tea party with the twins, I knew your future was assured. I even took Brigit aside that night for a pot of tea and found out more about her. While you were busy denying the truth, I was getting to know my future sister-in-law."

"If you were so certain, why did you keep shoving those other women at me?"

"Contrast. It was simple contrast." Emily gave him a mysterious smile. "It's taken you far too long to see the jewel that was right under your nose."

"Then stop delaying it further. I have a plan. You can help me."

❧

Brigit knew Duncan's new vessel was finished. Emily planned a christening the day after Christmas, and the ship would then go on her maiden voyage. That day couldn't come fast enough.

He'd thought her guilty. Aye, he had. Once she'd gotten a chance to think back, Brigit came to the galling realization that Duncan had been doing everything he could to set her up and capture her—he'd been trying to charm her, make her feel safe. He'd shared in her tea party and piano lesson with the twins. He'd discussed books—oh. Her heart twisted at the memory of how he'd toyed with her. He'd asked her about what punishment was appropriate for a thief!

And to think she'd actually fancied him a bit. That stung even worse. She'd given him her trust, and he'd barged right into every activity he could to find her weaknesses. The man was a scoundrel.

At least I didn't make my feelings known. I don't have to be humiliated that way. Sure and certain as can be, I'll never think of him favorably again. It may well be my job to serve the whole family, and I'll do it to the best of my ability, but I don't have to waste my breath talking to him.

❧

Duncan thought it quite telling that he had such cooperation with his scheme. Aye, the children thoroughly approved. He didn't have to give them the name of the lass whose heart he wanted to net. They all guessed, and he didn't bother to deny a word.

It hadn't taken much at all to enlist their help. Duncan simply went out and came home with an armful of mistletoe. He'd no more than walked in the door, and Lily peered down at him from the second floor. Her face lit with glee. "I'll fetch Anna Kathleen. We'll help!"

In almost no time at all, she and Anna tied the mistletoe into dainty little balls and sprigs. Timothy and Titus came over to investigate what they were doing and offered to help Duncan tack up the mistletoe in every doorway. It was gratifying, knowing they supported his plan.

Timothy stood back and stared at their handiwork. He

smirked and elbowed Titus. "Our Duncan's a man on a mission."

"I'm thinking it's a dangerous one," Anna chimed in as she looked up at the doorway where they'd just hung the last sprig. Her brows puckered; then she stood on tiptoe to straighten out a twisted ribbon. While Duncan wondered how she'd managed to turn into a fastidious young woman under his very nose, Anna gave him a pitying look. "Brigit's good and mad. I don't blame her one bit."

"I can't see why." Titus propped his hands on his slim hips.

"He's too young to understand." Lily tilted her nose at a superior angle.

"Hey. I'm older than you are!"

Lily gave her brother a hopeless look and shook her head so emphatically, her dark curls bounced. "What woman would want a man who didn't court her?"

"He's got mistletoe all over the house. She can't possibly miss it."

"Worse," Anna said softly, "what woman would want a man who didn't believe in her?"

"What kids wouldn't want some of Cook's gingerbread?" Duncan pointed toward the kitchen. "I'll bet you could talk her into letting you have some. Can't you smell it?"

They went off to the kitchen, but Duncan stayed behind and scowled at a small, fuzzy mistletoe leaf on the floor. Anna's words troubled Duncan. *Does Brigit think I don't believe in her?*

Never a man to stand by and do nothing once a problem was identified, Duncan sought Brigit at once. *At least this time, Emily won't call her away.* That thought did him no good. Duncan methodically searched the house from attic to basement and couldn't find the woman. Out of frustration he finally pulled Emily away from the piano teacher who was discussing music selections for the girls as if the decisions were of the gravest importance.

"I wasn't done yet," Emily protested.

"You can go back in a second. Just tell me where Brigit is."

"Oh, Mama needed her." Emily patted his arm reassuringly. "Da came by this morning and asked if Brigit couldn't help out. According to him, Mama and Brigit had some last-minute details to do on a Christmas gift."

Duncan yanked on his coat and headed for the door. Goodhew nodded and opened the door as he murmured, "Happy hunting, Sir."

"Practically broke my knuckles, dragging her back to the main house, so where does she go? Back to the cottage," Duncan muttered to himself. "The woman's a thief after all. She's robbed me of my sanity."

"She's robbed you of your heart, if I might say so."

Duncan gave Goodhew an exasperated grin. "You may not say so—even if you are twice my age and a valued person to my family."

"Close to thrice your age." Goodhew's mouth and cheeks looked as impassive as his voice sounded, but his eyes sparkled with merriment.

"I'm going to go talk some sense into my woman."

"You're a better man than I am, Sir. I've been married thirty-five years and have yet to accomplish that feat, but it is good to hear you call Miss Brigit, your woman, Sir."

Duncan left without another word. He marched down the road to the caretaker's cottage and noticed John had already managed to get the door replaced. Worried about Brigit when he kicked it in, Duncan hadn't given a thought to the damage, so the whole thing lasted only one slim day after the scuffle ere it turned into kindling. The new one looked sturdy, but he didn't bother to knock.

"Well, what a lovely surprise!" His mother smiled up at him.

Duncan glanced about and folded his arms akimbo. "Enough of you women conspiring against me. Where did you put her?"

"I haven't put anyone anywhere. Would you like a cup of tea?"

"I want Brigit. Em said she's here, and I'm tired of this game. Where is she?"

"Oh, Brigit was here this morning. She's such a lovely girl—talented, too. Did you see the wondrous tablecloth she embroidered for the twins? A tea-party tablecloth, she called it. Said they—"

"Mama, you can sing praises about Brigit's talents another day. Tell me where she's gone."

Da wandered in. "Why, didn't you know? Em's good about making sure her maids have days off, she is. Thoughtful. Little Brigit is thoughtful, too. Did your mama tell you—"

"Where is Brigit?" Duncan didn't want to be rude, but he'd lost what little patience he had.

"The lass said this is her afternoon off."

Duncan headed out the door. Barely containing his frustration, he managed to shut instead of slam it—but only because he respected his parents so much. *Tim wasn't wrong one bit— I'm a man on a mission.* He momentarily wished he'd ridden a horse and knew he could easily go to the stable to fetch one, but a walk would settle him down. In his present frame of mind, he'd likely scare the wits right out of Brigit. *I've been operating under a grave misconception, and all it accomplished was to muddy the waters. Now that I've figured out the problem, I'm going to solve it—just as soon as I catch up with that woman.*

❧

"Brigit."

Brigit froze when she heard her name. She'd been holding Da's arm, listening to him as they walked out of the ramshackle tenement building. Everything in her rebelled. She refused to turn.

"Why, now who's that handsome lad callin' out your name?" Da stepped forward a bit and took a good gander at Duncan.

Oh, she'd stuck to her guns and not taken the slightest peep at who had spoken—but she'd know Duncan's voice anywhere. "It's cold out, Da. Let's get going."

To her consternation, her father didn't budge. Duncan did. He came on over and shook her father's hand. "Duncan O'Brien, Sir. I'll be wanting to speak with you about your daughter just as soon as I talk with her a bit."

Her father tapped the toe of his boot on the ground. "Oh, so that's the way of it, is it?"

Brigit finally looked up at Duncan. She glowered at him; he winked. "He's a rascal, Da. Don't waste your breath."

"Of course he's a rascal. What with a fine Irish name like O'Brien, I'd have to expect as much. He can't be all bad if he's taking a liking to you."

"Da!"

"I came to walk her home, Sir."

"Now there's a fine man. Manners. Protective." Da nodded approvingly. His eyes narrowed. "Just whose home?"

"The Newcombs. Emily Newcomb is my sister."

Da's chuckle made Brigit's stomach churn. He gave her a bit of a squeeze. "This Duncan's something, all right. Everyone knows John Newcomb owns the shipyard, and your young man's standing here—"

"He's not my young man!"

Her father tilted her face up to his and said softly, "I know you too well, Daughter. Your strong reaction tells me you hold some feelings for the man, and his presence here tells me plenty."

A scalding wave of embarrassment washed over her. "Da!"

"From what I see, the pair of you need to settle a wee bit of a tiff."

"We'll get things worked out, Mr. Murphy." Duncan took hold of her other hand.

She snatched it back.

Da gave her a kiss. "Off with you now. Be happy."

Brigit watched in shock as her father walked back inside, effectively abandoning her.

twenty-two

"It's cold out. Let's get going."

Brigit jolted. "Don't you dare repeat my words and use them against me."

"Do you want me to hire a ride for us, or would you rather walk?"

"Both." She flashed him a heated look. "We'll each do one of those."

"We'll walk. The chilly air might cool your temper." He said the words so blandly, the scoundrel managed to get a fair hold of her arm and start leading her off before she even realized what he'd done.

Brigit dug in her heels and hissed, "I need my job. You're going to spoil it all."

"If you'd cooperate even the least little bit, that wouldn't be a problem."

She let out a longsuffering sigh. "You're making a scene, and the only way I'll make it through is simply to go along. It doesn't mean I have to talk to you at all."

"That's fine." They started to walk again, and he added, "I'll be happy to do all the talking."

Brigit quickened her pace. "You're impossible. The next thing I know, you'll be blaming all of this on me because I helped you escape that day. I can't regret it, though. No, I don't. I spared those lasses being married off to the likes of you. You would have broken their tender hearts."

"I'm thinkin' you're the one with the tender heart, Brigit."

"Can't you just leave me alone?"

He curled his hand around her. "No."

Brigit could feel tears burning behind her eyes. She refused to cry. "Let go of me. I declare, if I weren't such a lady, I'd smack you."

"I can see I'm perfectly safe then. It's clear as a cloudless sky that you're a lady."

"Don't you try to be charming, Captain O'Brien. I won't fall for it. No, I most certainly won't. I already know the truth."

"What truth is that?"

"Shakespeare said it quite well in Hamlet: A man can smile and smile and still be a villain." Brigit moaned and braced her forehead with one hand as she stared at the slushy ground. *I can't believe I said that to him. Oh, dear Lord above, I'm digging myself a grave here. If I say another word, I'll likely lose my job.*

"So I'm a villain."

Brigit didn't reply. She concentrated on the toes of her shoes. The hem of her blue dress was getting a wee bit damp. Snow had fallen very briefly today and promptly melted at the edge of the path. Not that it should matter. She really didn't care a whit about her appearance. It wasn't as if she wanted to impress anyone—especially Duncan.

They walked in silence for a ways. Duncan shot her a bold look and mused aloud again, "So I'm a villain. What is my crime?"

"You've stolen my peace of mind," Brigit snapped. She lifted her arms in the air in an impatient, flinging gesture and started to walk faster still. "I can't believe you just prodded me into admitting that. Don't you dare act as if it just happened, because you planned it. You're a man who plots his course carefully, so I know you meant to hound me. Didn't anyone ever teach you it's rude to provoke a woman?" She groaned. She'd told him she wasn't going to speak to him, and here she was, babbling. "If I speak to you any longer, someone is going to certify me a lunatic."

"I could lock you in the attic. The door sometimes sticks. No, wait. I can't do that. You'd end up breaking your neck, climbing out on the roof."

"Your humor is—"

"To mask how I've lost my own peace."

Brigit cast a glance at him and burst into tears. "You dreadful man. Don't you even begin thinking I feel the smallest scrap of pity for you."

"I don't want your pity; I want your forgiveness."

When she started crying, she'd lost track of where she was going. Brigit plowed into a bush, and Duncan yanked her back and turned her around. He opened his greatcoat, pulled her to his chest, and wrapped her in his arms and warmth. He held her while she soaked his shirt with tears.

Brigit sucked in a choppy breath and managed to hiccup in the most unladylike way as she let it out. She muttered against Duncan's chest, "'Tis said God watches out for children and fools. He surely must be watching me now. Honest and true, I've made a fool of myself sobbing like a baby."

"God is nigh, my sweet. I have no doubt of that. I've been calling upon Him to help straighten out this mess, and it's time we talk. I've hurt you badly, and I'm sorry to the marrow of my bones for that."

Brigit wiggled out of his arms. Duncan promptly shed his coat and draped it around her shoulders. He held it there by wrapping his arm about her and nudging her to walk.

"I've plenty to say and am trying to decide where to begin. I was so busy fighting Emily's matchmaking plans that I closed my eyes to any woman. When I took the lads on that voyage with me, I was miserable. Oh—'twasn't on account of them. 'Twas because from the first time I set foot on a Newcomb ship, I've loved to go to sea. That whole trip I didn't find a moment's pleasure with sailing. All I did was think of you."

Brigit trudged on in silence.

"By the time I came back, I'd determined you were all I could ever hope for in a bride—a solid Christian woman, you lit up the room when you came in, and you lit up my heart. I nearly kissed you during that snow fight on Phillip's birthday, but I came to my senses in time. I didn't want to give anyone call to cast aspersions on our character."

He stepped over a fallen branch and lifted her over. Before he set her back down, Duncan waited until Brigit looked into his eyes. Sincerity shone in the depths of his eyes. "I'm ashamed of what I'll be saying next, but I cannot ask forgiveness if I don't confess."

Brigit bit her lip and nodded.

Duncan tucked her close to his side, and they continued toward home. "John and Emily told me we had a thief. They'd narrowed down the possibilities until 'twas one of the maids. We talked long into the night. The Bible says perfect love casts out fear. My love for you was far from perfect; and as John and I started to piece together the facts, they all pointed at you."

"I never did anything!"

"I know." He sighed. "A book and a fountain pen were taken. Trudy and Fiona can't read or write. Since Trudy started acting moon-eyed, Em always assigned her to work with someone else, so we knew she couldn't have taken the fan or cameo. Fiona is too clumsy to sneak into any room unnoticed, though we agreed she spends a fair amount of time with the twins and might have taken the doll."

"Phillip admitted he took the doll."

"Sure and enough, Brigit, he did. The problem was, we didn't know that at the time. Nothing had ever been stolen until you started working for John and Emily. That alone weighed heavily against you. Worst of all, you'd discovered the little shepherdess statue was missing; but then I saw you with a bundle. You stopped outside your parents' building and boasted about having things to please your mother."

"Cook gave me apricots for M—" She stopped herself, then shrieked, "You followed me?!"

"Shhh. I'd gone to vote and saw you walking down the street. At the time I needed to figure out where your father was so I could ask him for your hand—so, yes, I did follow you. At the last minute I recalled a promise I'd made to Em. I told her when I found the right woman, she'd be the first to know. I couldn't very well break my word, so I came home. I went to her, but that's when she and John told me about the missing things."

"So instead you condemned me for being a thief and wanted to chop off my hand." Every last word made her tight throat ache.

"All of the evidence was there, Brigit. Wrong as it turned out to be, it stacked up against you. By now you know how Edward hornswoggled my sister Anna into a sham marriage. I hadn't recovered from that. My pride had me believing you'd been hurting my family right under my nose. The betrayal I felt cut deep. When I saw you on the roof, the last flicker of hope I'd held got snuffed out."

"So now you think to woo me? No, Duncan. I don't want a man who cannot hold more faith in me than that."

"That's where you're wrong."

Brigit closed her eyes in horror. She'd just presumed far too much and humiliated herself. Duncan wouldn't let her pull away, though.

"I looked into your eyes that night and knew deep in my heart that you couldn't have stolen a thing. I went against John's orders and took you to my parents. I wanted you to be sheltered until I could solve the mystery. All along I tried to prove to you that I stood by your side. I came by each day. I made sure you still got your salary, and the household staff figured you were special because I'd chosen you to go help my mama. I even put that Bible verse in the sewing box for you."

"You did that? The verse came from you?"

"Aye, Brigit. I wanted to encourage you. Until I cleared your name, I had no right to speak my heart. I was trying my hardest to brace you up, but I've come to see you didn't understand."

"How could I? You'd been trying to trap me all along. I thought you were hovering just to scare me because you thought I'd betray your parents."

Duncan groaned. "I'm accustomed to working on a ship with a crew of men. As it turns out, I'm none too good at figuring out how a woman thinks."

They'd finally arrived at the back of the estate. Duncan turned her to face out over the ocean. Ships bobbed along the dock. "God's given me a love for you, Brigit Murphy. It's big as the ocean. Our ship went through a mighty storm and got stuck on treacherous shoals. Tide's coming in, and I want our ship to float free. With your forgiveness and God's blessing, we could sail through life together." He turned loose of her and walked around so he stood directly in front of her. Taking her hand in his, he knelt right in a thin layer of ice. "I'm not just asking your forgiveness, Brigit. I'm asking for your hand and your heart. I love you, Lass. Marry me."

The door flew open, and Titus dashed out. "Don't you hear the bells? Come on!"

"Bells?" Duncan and Brigit repeated the word in unison.

"Hurry. Dad and Tim are saddling horses." Titus slapped Duncan on the arm. "The church is on fire!"

❧

Brigit clutched Emily's hand and bowed her head. "Heavenly Father, please watch over our men. Keep them safe. Oh, please keep them safe. A pretty church can be rebuilt, but a fine man—I can't replace Duncan. I'm asking You not to take him away from me just when You've brought our hearts together. Be with Mr. John and Timothy and Titus and all the other men, too. . . ."

After praying, Brigit sat in the kitchen with Emily, sharing a pot of tea. She spent considerably more time stirring her cup than drinking from it. The grandfather clock chimed the quarter hour, and she remarked on the obvious. "They're still not back."

Emily said nothing.

"I'm worried," Brigit confessed. "Duncan is there—he could get hurt. I'm supposing I ought to have faith; but the truth is, faith isn't a shield against bad things happening."

A melancholy smile chased across Emily's face. "That's true. Believers still have problems. Sickness and death visit their homes."

Brigit took a gulp of tea and stared at the rim of the cup. The tea had grown tepid, and she couldn't even warm her hands around the cup. "I can't imagine living with the worry and not having God to lean on. I'm scared, but I know He's with Duncan right now—and with Mr. John and your sons."

"And the Lord is with us, too." Emily stood and added more hot water to the teapot. "Love puts your heart at risk. There's always the danger of the one you love hurting you or being hurt. The thing that gets us through is knowing that grace redeems us. Whether it's God's grace and forgiveness through Christ or the forgiveness we grant one another, it's what gives us another chance."

"The way Duncan gave me another chance, even when I looked guilty."

"And the way you've forgiven his doubts."

The cup clinked softly as Brigit put it on her saucer. "My father is fond of telling me nothing good comes easy. If he's right, I'm supposing my marriage to Duncan ought to be the finest ever."

Emily cried out delightedly, "He asked? I thought maybe he hadn't had a chance to propose yet."

Brigit started to giggle. "Aye, he asked. But I didn't have a chance to answer him before he ran off. Should I be wondering if he'll keep running in the opposite direction now that he'll have a chance to reconsider his offer?"

"Not at all. If anything, that'll bring him back. You've given him every reason to come home."

They went through another pot of tea. The clock chimed again. And again.

"Even with the rough start you've had, you and Duncan are a good match." Emily smiled. "You've both lived through being rich and poor; you both love the Lord and want to serve Him, and the very height of emotions that sparks between you proves much is possible—if only you give it a chance."

"I do want to. Just as we were saying: God set the example; forgiveness grants the gift of redemption."

"That's right." Emily sweetened her next cup of tea. "John and I stayed up late into the night talking about that very thing. He tracked down Edward today."

"Well, praise be!"

"Duncan sent a wee gift along—he and I decided Edward ought to have the little golden hearts on the red cord that he'd given to our Anna. John told me Edward was speechless."

Cook walked into the kitchen. "The gentlemen are back and stabling their mounts. I presume they'll be hungry."

The front door opened. "Brigit!" Duncan yelled.

"Oh, dear. Now what did I do?" She stood up.

Emily rose and pushed her toward the entryway. "From the way that brother of mine is bellowing, the whole world is about to find out."

Soot-covered and disheveled, Duncan was halfway up the stairs. "Where is she?"

"I'm down here," Brigit called.

He jumped over the banister and strode up to her. "Before I raced off, I asked you a question, Lass. I haven't heard an answer."

"The church burned down," Timothy advised. "If you always wanted a church wedding, you'd best tell him no. He's too impatient to wait for them to rebuild."

"He ran into the church and carried out the altar." John chuckled. "That ought to count for something."

"They're pests, but I love them." Duncan took her by the hands and started to pull her toward the parlor so they could have some privacy. "Putting up with me might be hard, but do you think you can stand them?"

"I love you, Duncan O'Brien. I'll gladly wed you and take them in the bargain."

"He got her under the mistletoe!"

"Fitting it is, too," Emily said. "She'll be a Christmas bride."

Brigit didn't hear another thing because Duncan took her in his arms and kissed her senseless.

epilogue

"Mr. Duncan asked that his bride be given this." Goodhew stood in the doorway and handed Emily an envelope. He stood on tiptoe, looked over Emily's head, and smiled. "And might I say, Miss Brigit, you look radiant."

"Thank you."

"Everything is ready downstairs. Mrs. Murphy, the cloth you stitched for the altar is exquisite. It covered the burned edge so no one can see the singe marks at all."

Brigit's mother beamed. "'Tis kind of you to be saying so."

Nonny and Emily both fussed with one last bow on Brigit's gown. They'd been stitching it in secret since Duncan brought back the satin from his trip to Lowell.

Brigit waited until Goodhew escorted Nonny, Emily, and Mum out; then she opened the note.

Beloved Brigit,

The day John married Emily, he gave me a shiny new quarter to signify that I was one-fourth of their family. Through the years, it's been a reminder to me that I was wanted. I've enclosed a brand-new gold Indian Princess dollar. I'm trading up. You are my whole world, my princess, and our future is golden. Let it serve as the first of many reminders that you are loved, my bride.

—D

Late that evening Duncan carried his bride across the gangplank and onto the *Redeemed*. Just yesterday the bride had christened the vessel. Tonight the captain's cabin would be their honeymoon suite. In two days the *Redeemed* would go on her maiden voyage, carrying cotton to Ireland. In accordance with the family tradition, the bride would sail with her groom.

Anna Kathleen had caught the bridal bouquet, and she'd tossed it back into the carriage as Duncan and Brigit departed. Brigit put the bouquet down on the table in the cabin, and it made an odd sound.

"What was that sound?" Duncan looked around.

"It's a wedding wish."

"Oh?" He wrapped his arms around her waist and nuzzled her temple.

Brigit urged, "Look at the ribbon on my flowers."

"I'd rather look at you."

"'Tis the coin you sent me. I tied it to my flowers for our wedding."

"And God tied our hearts together at the altar. I'm going to love you forever, Brigit-mine."

A Letter To Our Readers

Dear Reader:

In order that we might better contribute to your reading enjoyment, we would appreciate your taking a few minutes to respond to the following questions. We welcome your comments and read each form and letter we receive. When completed, please return to the following:

Fiction Editor
Heartsong Presents
PO Box 719
Uhrichsville, Ohio 44683

1. Did you enjoy reading *Redeemed Hearts* by Cathy Marie Hake?
   ❏ Very much! I would like to see more books by this author!
   ❏ Moderately. I would have enjoyed it more if

   _____

   _____

   _____

2. Are you a member of **Heartsong Presents**? ❏ Yes ❏ No
   If no, where did you purchase this book? _____

   _____

3. How would you rate, on a scale from 1 (poor) to 5 (superior), the cover design? _____

4. On a scale from 1 (poor) to 10 (superior), please rate the following elements.

   ____ Heroine   ____ Plot
   ____ Hero   ____ Inspirational theme
   ____ Setting   ____ Secondary characters

5. These characters were special because?_____

_____

_____

6. How has this book inspired your life?_____

_____

_____

7. What settings would you like to see covered in future
   Heartsong Presents books? _____

_____

_____

8. What are some inspirational themes you would like to see
   treated in future books? _____

_____

_____

9. Would you be interested in reading other **Heartsong
   Presents** titles? ❏ Yes ❏ No

10. Please check your age range:
    ❏ Under 18   ❏ 18-24
    ❏ 25-34   ❏ 35-45
    ❏ 46-55   ❏ Over 55

Name_____

Occupation _____

Address _____

City_____ State_____ Zip_____

CHURCH IN THE WILDWOOD

4 stories in 1

*F*or four generations, the citizens of Hickory Hollow, Missouri, have gathered for worship in the valley's little brown church. Many a soul has found salvation amid this blissful country scene. . .and more than a few lonely hearts have met their true love while seated on the chapel's pew.

Authors: Paige Winship Dooly, Kristy Dykes, Pamela Griffin, and Debby Mayne.

Historical, paperback, 352 pages, 5 $^{3}/_{16}$"x 8"

❤ ❤ ❤ ❤ ❤ ❤ ❤ ❤ ❤ ❤ ❤ ❤ ❤ ❤ ❤

❤ ❤ ❤ ❤ ❤ ❤ ❤ ❤ ❤ ❤ ❤ ❤ ❤ ❤ ❤

Presents